Trying to correct the mistake, Richard began to move towards Steven while speaking. Steven watched him, grateful for his help, and then suddenly out of the corner of his eye he saw one of the huge flats start to wobble. For the briefest of moments it trembled as though in a breeze and then, as Steven gave a shout of horror, the top began to slant towards the stage until, with a terrible groaning noise, the entire structure over-balanced and crashed face down onto the stage.

In the few brief seconds that the incident took to happen, they all ran for their lives. They bumped into each other, screamed, pushed and tried frantic-ally to get out of the way. Then, as the whole stage shook beneath the shock of the crushing weight they stood in the wings, their eyes huge in their pale faces as they checked to see they'd all got safely clear. They hadn't. Beneath the huge white flat one of the group now lay hidden from view, silenced for ever.

P●INT CRIME

A DRAMATIC DEATH

Margaret Bingley

Cover illustration by David Wyatt

SCHOLASTIC

Scholastic Children's Books,
Scholastic Publications Ltd,
7–9 Pratt Street, London NW1 0AE, UK

Scholastic Inc.,
555 Broadway, New York, NY 10012-3999, USA

Scholastic Canada Ltd,
123 Newkirk Road, Richmond Hill,
Ontario, Canada L4C 3G5

Ashton Scholastic Pty Ltd,
P O Box 579, Gosford, New South Wales,
Australia

Ashton Scholastic Ltd,
Private Bag 92801, Penrose, Auckland,
New Zealand

First published in the UK by Scholastic Publications Ltd, 1994

Text copyright © Margaret Bingley, 1994

Cover illustration copyright © David Wyatt, 1994

ISBN 0 590 55490 5

Typeset by TW Typesetting, Midsomer Norton, Avon
Printed by Cox & Wyman Ltd, Reading, Berks

10 9 8 7 6 5 4 3 2 1

Prologue

It was only first thing in the morning that it showed. Then, for a few brief minutes the face that was reflected in the wardrobe mirror at the foot of the bed was not the same as the face that the rest of the world saw. The difference was subtle, but it was there.

While vestiges of sleep still clogged the brain, the eyes shifted restlessly from side to side, as the disturbed mind tried to adjust to the new day. At night, in dreams, the pain and anger felt by the damaged mind would surface. Dreadful nightmares plagued the long, dark hours; nightmares in which the reality of the harm that had been done roamed free.

In those early waking moments, the mouth too

was different. The lips were tight and angry, and sometimes, as the mouth stretched in a yawn, a small hissing sound of rage would escape.

If anyone had seen the face as it was then, they would have known. The terror that had become part of their small community ever since the accidents began would have been brought to an end, because the sight of the face would have clearly exposed the sick and twisted mind behind it all. But there never were any witnesses.

For those first few minutes of the day, the face was safe. Then, after the normal routine of washing and teeth cleaning, everything would be under control again. The demons of the night were locked away during daylight hours, the eyes no longer shifted in their sockets and the mouth was a perfectly normal mouth.

The mask was on. The face could now fit in. No one would know. But behind the mask the sickness was still there, lurking just beneath the surface and far beyond all control.

Every morning, as the reflection faded from the bathroom mirror, the mirror would cloud over for a moment. The mask had that effect on people too. It clouded their judgement.

That was why they were all still in such great danger.

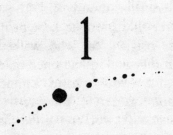

1

It was the first full rehearsal of The Dorking Future Drama Group's latest production, and as usual this meant total chaos.

"Hey, look at Becky's hair!" Suzanne exclaimed to Emma, her closest friend.

Emma looked and began to giggle. "Talk about her crowning glory! Perhaps she's put it up in case she marries an aristocrat and has to wear tiaras!"

Just then Richard bounded up to them. "Want to see the sketch I've done of you two?"

"Not much," muttered Suzanne.

"Come on, I did it in five minutes, see."

The friends looked at his wickedly clever cartoon of them, heads together over a cauldron like two witches.

"Very clever," said Emma. "Try doing yourself. A clown's nose would suit you."

Richard grinned. "You girls have no sense of humour."

"You're just not funny," said Claire, coming up behind him. A thin, moody girl, she was a good actress but her sharp tongue kept people at arm's length. "The original cat who walked by itself," Suzanne's brother Steven had once called her.

"Did he draw you?" asked Emma, then fell against Suzanne as Hazel, the overweight, none-too-bright backstage worker pushed past her with some scenery, accidentally hitting her full in the back as she passed.

"Look out!" Suzanne exclaimed.

Hazel blushed. "Sorry! I thought I'd got room."

"She's so thick!" muttered Claire.

"She's okay," Emma retorted, rubbing the top of her arm. "At least she's keen, always here for every rehearsal. I quite like her."

"I didn't realize you were into charity work," remarked Claire. "She drives me up the wall, and so does Richard. Just listen to him!"

On the other side of the room, Richard was entertaining Steven and his friend Stuart with his drawings, laughing loudly at each one. "This one of Claire's good," said Steven, admiring the sleek leopard with Claire's unmistakable features.

"She didn't think so," laughed Richard. "Stuart,

have you got round to asking Suzanne out yet? I can always do it for you!"

"Do shut up," hissed Stuart. "She'll hear you."

"I think she knows you're keen," commented Suzanne's brother. "She isn't blind, and you never stop staring at her."

"You stare at Becky," retorted Stuart.

"Everyone stares at Becky – she's the best-looking babe for miles!" said Richard. As usual he spoke loudly, and all the girls in the rehearsal room heard him.

Becky, who was well aware that her auburn hair, green eyes and incredible figure were her greatest assets because academically she was hopeless, smiled and checked that her hair was still in place on top of her head.

Claire, Emma and Suzanne turned to glare at Richard, but he was busy entertaining his friends with an imitation of a tutor at his art college and didn't notice.

"He's a total idiot," said Claire. "Even if he becomes a famous artist I shan't let on I ever knew him."

"He's not that bad!" protested Suzanne. "He likes making people laugh, that's all."

"He's never once made me laugh," retorted Claire before stalking off to get ready for the beginning of the rehearsal.

"Pity she doesn't make us laugh sometimes,"

said Emma to Suzanne. "By the way, Suzie, is Steven going out with Liza?" She made her voice casual, but Suzanne knew only too well that like most of the girls Emma fancied Steven like mad.

"No, he's too busy studying – he did take her out a couple of times but she wanted to 'get serious', which terrified him," Suzie assured her friend.

Just then, Mike, the producer, yelled at them all to shut up and get ready to do some work.

"I've had Dad shouting at me all morning because he thinks I should be studying this afternoon. Now I come here to act, and Mike shouts in his place," muttered Steven.

Stuart shrugged. "That's the trouble with being clever and artistic. Everyone wants you. If I don't get decent A Level grades no one will want me."

"Suzanne might!" Steven said.

"I thought you said she fancied Mike?"

"Yes, well she does, but she knows it's a waste of time really. You might be able to persuade her otherwise."

"Yeah, but if I ask and she says no, then I've blown it. I want to choose the right moment."

"If you're in the first Act, get on stage. If you're not, sit down somewhere and keep quiet!" bellowed Mike.

Lynne, who was in charge of props and generally indispensable backstage, hurried into the hall late,

4

with her arms full.

"Sorry!" she called sheepishly. "I thought we began at two-thirty."

Steven smiled at her. "Don't worry, all we've done's talk so far."

His smile was enough to make Lynne pleased she'd been late. She thought he was gorgeous but normally he hardly noticed her. "That's lucky," she mumbled, going red in the face.

"Get on stage!" roared Mike furiously.

At last order began to emerge from the chaos, the hall lights were dimmed and the rehearsal began.

Steven slipped quietly into a seat. Becky started prancing around on the stage, her beautiful face as blank as usual when she was acting, and her flat voice totally killing all the meaning in the lines. He grinned to himself. It was lucky his parents weren't here to see this. Becky was certainly no advert for the acting career he was determined to follow.

Not that Becky intended to be an actress. No, it was just because she was easily the most attractive girl in the group that she got all the parts that called for a "beautiful" girl. Her acting might make him groan, but he could still admire her looks and he had to go along with Richard's description of her. She was a real babe.

The other girls were all jealous of her, and Steven could see why. They were far better actresses than

Becky but even when Becky's parts in their productions were small it was her that the local paper would comment on.

"Becky Nicholls lit up the stage with her very presence", the critics had written the previous spring. Well, she certainly wasn't lighting up the stage at this moment, and even as Steven watched, Mike Lucas shouted at her from his seat directly in front of the stage.

"That's terrible, Becky!" he yelled. The other girls on the stage tried not to look pleased while Becky stared down at him in hurt surprise.

"You've just been given a kitten for a birthday present. *A kitten.* You are playing a seventeen-year-old girl who quite rightly considers herself far too old to get a kitten for a present. You are meant to look totally fed up, as angry as you dare to be, considering how strict your parents are. From where I'm sitting you look as though you've got a mild attack of indigestion. Would you please try and make this a little more convincing. This is a vital scene, the moment when you first start to stand up to your family, to show them that you're not a small girl any more. Just take a five-minute break and try and dig up some emotion from the depths of your tranquil little soul – right?"

Becky, her beautiful face slightly creased in bewilderment, nodded, but Steven could tell that she had no idea what Mike wanted from her. The lights came up and everyone began moving towards the flasks of coffee set on a table in the hall.

"That told her," said Suzanne to Steven as she joined him. "At last it's stopped her looking so smug."

"I can't see how she looks, I'm stuck in the prompt corner," said Emma, smiling at Steven.

"I thought you were in this scene," said Steven.

"Not till later and they need a prompt because Becky keeps forgetting her words."

"Makes you wonder why Mike picked her for the part," commented Steven.

"I picked her for the part because the character's meant to be outstandingly beautiful," said Mike, walking up to them. "Besides, the critics adore her, and we sell more tickets when she's got a good part."

"Anyone would think you were an accountant, not a producer," said Claire.

"Claire would have been much better in the part," Emma commented. "With make-up she could have looked just as good, and at least she can act." With that she turned on her heel and walked away.

"Ouch!" said Mike with a grin.

"You can't blame the other girls for feeling put out. Becky has to be the world's worst actress," remarked Steven.

Mike drew him to one side. "How are things at home?"

Steven shrugged. He wished everyone would leave him alone instead of trying to pull him in the direction they wanted. "The same as usual, but I'm not giving in. Once the A Levels are out of the way I'm writing off to drama schools."

"Good for you. Right, I'd better get everyone back on stage and see what I can do to improve this scene. Could be some time yet before we can move on."

Mike called for silence, the hall lights went out and the characters re-grouped on stage. Becky drifted around like a lovely doll while James Desmond, who was playing her father, stumbled through a long speech about how much trouble he'd taken choosing her birthday present with her mother, and how they hoped she'd like it. As he muddled on, Richard was making Hazel laugh in the wings until a glare from Claire stopped him.

"*Look excited!*" yelled Mike. "Begin to anticipate something really good. That will make the present of the kitten even more of an anti-climax."

Becky fluttered her hands around her face and widened her eyes.

"What's that supposed to mean?" Mike demanded. Steven hung his head and tried not to laugh. It wasn't Becky's fault, she simply couldn't reproduce genuine emotions on the stage. In fact, she rarely showed any in real life. She was content to drift along, secure in the power of her beauty. At this age it was all she needed.

After a couple more attempts Mike gave up. "All right. Let's move on to the actual giving of the present. Claire, when you hand her the box remember that deep down you know she won't like it. You're a manipulative woman, who doesn't want her daughter to grow up because it will take the attention away from you. The words don't tell the audience that in this scene, so use your face to do it instead."

Steven took more interest. Claire Elliott was probably the best actress in the group. He was interested to study the expression in her eyes as she handed the box, nicely gift-wrapped and containing a very cute toy kitten from the local toy shop, to her stage daughter. For a moment there was a gleam of genuine malice in her eyes, and although her mouth curved upwards in a smile it was a thin smile and her eyes conveyed the sentiments Mike had requested exactly. Yes, thought Steven, she was really good.

Becky took the box from her and faced the front of the stage. "Oh, how exciting," she said, in outstandingly bored tones. "I can hardly wait to open it."

Mike groaned. This was Becky at her worst.

She fiddled slowly with the ribbon, with no hint of excitement in the movements, and lifted the lid of the box. Then, to the amazement of everyone in the hall, she emitted the most terrible blood-curdling scream, dropped the box on the ground and bolted off-stage sobbing hysterically.

"A bit extreme, but pretty good all things considered!" laughed Mike.

Steven was impressed. It was over the top, but it showed that Becky *was* capable of showing deep emotion. It was only when all the others on the stage remained rooted to the spot, staring down at where the toy kitten was lying on the boards that he began to realize something was wrong. Then one of the girls began to cry and turned her head away, while the boys shuffled their feet uneasily.

"You'd better look at this, Mike," called Stuart, who was up on the stage. "It's pretty gross."

Mike hurried out of his seat, Steven following close behind him. By now all the girls were huddled together in a group, and a couple of them were in tears. The boys had stayed separate, their faces very pale.

"What is it? What's wrong?" demanded Mike.

Steven climbed the three steps to the stage and stared down at the "kitten". His stomach lurched and he had to swallow hard against the sickness in his throat; because when Becky had opened the box it was no toy that had met her eyes but, instead, a very dead cat. It now lay on the stage;

stiff, glassy-eyed and all too obviously the victim of a nasty road accident.

"Where did this come from?" demanded Mike furiously. "Who's in charge of props?"

"I am," said Lynne nervously.

"I put the toy kitten in the box," said Christine quietly. She was older than the others, nearly twenty-two, author of the play and Mike's long-standing girlfriend. "Lynne was late so I got it ready for the scene and put it down on the floor off-stage."

"And that's where it was when I collected it," said Claire, detaching herself from the group of shaken girls. "I thought it felt a bit heavy, but it's only in my hands for a few seconds before I give it to Becky."

"Well, whoever put this thing inside the box has to have a pretty sick sense of humour," said Mike angrily. "Someone get a plastic bag or something. I'll take it home and bury it in my garden. We'll call it a day after this. Christine, can you go and find Becky and try and calm her down? It must have given her a dreadful shock. As for the rest of you, all I can say is this:

"Playing this kind of trick isn't funny, it's cruel and if I ever find out who the culprit is they'll be out of the group immediately. As for the future, there must never be anything like it again or I'll close the whole group down, is that understood?"

They all nodded, struck dumb by the shock and the unpleasant realization of the deliberate cruelty that lay behind the incident.

"Right, off you all go. As tomorrow's Sunday we'll begin rehearsing at one-thirty and work until five. There's still a lot of work to get through before this is ready for the paying public. Now remember to check all doors and windows before you leave."

Slowly everyone drifted away. Christine took Becky home in her car while everyone else hurried to collect their things and go. No one wanted to look at the dead cat still lying stiffly on the stage and they were all relieved when Mike finally put it into a bag and took it away with him.

"Who would want to do something like that?" Suzanne asked Steven as she and Emma walked home with him.

"A lot of you girls resent Becky. I suppose it could have been a spiteful way of making her react more realistically," said Steven, who was more shaken than he was letting on.

"You'd have to be really sick to think of something like that though," said Emma. "Imagine, someone had to collect that dead cat and put it in the box – ugh!"

The three of them fell silent, all wondering who in the group was capable of doing such a thing.

2

By nine o'clock on the Sunday morning, a disgruntled Steven was already working. He was taking English Literature, Art and History at A Level, but as all he wanted to do was act he resented the time revision took up. It also left him with very little social life, since Mike seemed to want him at rehearsals whenever he was free.

Suddenly Suzanne put her head round the door. "Emma and I are off to the rehearsal hall in half an hour. Mike's just rung to say that he wants everyone possible to go along and start putting the set up. Since I'm lucky enough not to be a genius, I can go!"

Steven looked at his sister and laughed. "I didn't know you were that keen on putting up scenery!"

Suzanne blushed. She wasn't. It was Mike she was keen on, as her brother knew. "I like the atmosphere," she said defensively.

"And the producer! You must be daft, Stuart's dead keen on you. Mike hardly knows you're there except when you're acting."

Suzanne stuck out her tongue. "Just because Stuart's your friend it doesn't mean I have to like him too. All he talks about is these wonderful films he's going to make in the future. Some hope!"

"I thought Emma was behind with her GCSE assignments. How come she's able to go?"

Suzanne shrugged. "You know how it is at her place since her mum re-married. Emma's only too keen to find any excuse to get out." She hesitated, wondering whether she should mention her friend's passion for Steven but decided against it. He probably knew anyway. "You know that dead cat?" she said slowly.

Steven raised his head and saw the fear on his sister's face. "Forget it!" he said forcefully. "Someone wanted to upset Becky and they succeeded. It won't happen again."

"But *who* would do it?" demanded Suzanne.

"I don't think I want to know," admitted Steven.

"It has to have been one of the group, one of our friends. I've been thinking about it and I just can't believe any of us could have done it, but they did. It makes me feel uncomfortable about today's rehearsal," confessed Suzanne.

"I know what you mean, but I guess everyone feels the same."

"Not quite everyone. Whoever did it won't be worried," Suzanne pointed out as she left her brother reluctantly studying.

Emma was waiting for Suzanne outside her front door. "I'm glad Mike rang," she confessed. "Can you hear that child yelling in there?"

"That child" was Emma's new five-year-old step-sister Paula, and Suzanne could clearly hear her yelling. "It would drive me mad," she said sympathetically, "but I suppose we all shrieked a lot at that age."

"If I threw temper tantrums I got smacked. Mum just tries to distract Paula. She says it's a better way to handle her – huh! When's Steven coming?" she added as casually as she could manage.

"This afternoon. It's hard being brain of Britain and a budding actor! What do you think of my outfit?"

"The jeans are a bit tight for shifting great chunks of scenery around! There's no point in trying to impress Mike, Suzie. He's going out with Christine: they're almost engaged."

When they arrived, Mike and Stuart were already hard at work constructing a doorway. Suzanne noticed Stuart smiling at her and smiled back. She had to admit he was rather attractive – she liked the way his brown hair fell over one eye, however hard he tried to keep it pushed back.

Becky was also there. Her skin-tight, shocking pink leggings were topped by a black and pink ribbed jersey with a deep V-neck. She looked more like someone about to go to a party than a back-stage worker.

As usual Christine was hard at work. She and James Desmond were busy working on the ropes that were to pull the large "flats" into place. These were heavy rectangular wooden frames covered in painted canvas. At the moment they were plain white, but once upright would be painted to form the walls of the living room where most of the action took place. Each of the three pieces was some 2.5 metres high. Getting them into place needed great care and skill, which was why both Christine and Mike had to be there to supervise. Mike, who was a trained drama teacher and worked at the local girls' school, was always acutely safety conscious. Once the flats were up, Mike joined Christine and together they checked the knots.

"No Claire?" asked Emma during a brief break for coffee.

"She hates this kind of work," replied Stuart. "It's just the acting she cares about. I enjoy both; if you work in rep, you have to do everything."

"That's fine by me," remarked Mike. "She's good enough to concentrate on the acting side alone."

"But not good enough to get the best part in this play!" whispered Suzanne to Emma. They both glanced across to where Becky was sitting close to Mike. Becky caught the look and promptly ran her fingers through her long hair and laughed vivaciously at something Mike had said.

"Stupid show-off!" muttered Emma.

After the break ended, Hazel arrived. Emma, noticing that no one bothered to say hello, went over to her. "Hi! Perhaps now you're here some work'll get done." Hazel blushed in surprised pleasure, while Lynne, who'd been working hard for an hour on her own, glared at Emma.

"Why did you say that? She's useless!" exclaimed Suzanne.

"I felt sorry for her. After all, unlike Claire she *is* here."

At twelve o'clock the flats were securely in place and James had begun painting them. A bookcase was put on stage, to be filled later by book jackets wrapped round blocks of board.

Everyone ate the sandwiches that Christine had provided, and shortly afterwards the rest of the members turned up and started talking about whether or not they'd learned their lines. Richard claimed not to know any and went around quaking with mock terror and quoting other people's lines.

Suzanne and Emma were about to go up on stage when James joined them. He was short, with the long hair that seemed to be compulsory at art school. Quite apart from his artistic skills he was a reasonable character actor, but unfortunately imagined that he bore a resemblance to Mel Gibson, and longed for romantic lead roles.

"Are you going to the bowling alley tonight?" he asked Emma abruptly.

Suzanne tried not to giggle at the look on her friend's face. "I don't know," said Emma stonily. "It depends on who else goes."

"I wondered if you'd like to go with me?" James suggested.

"No thanks."

James flushed. "What do you mean, no thanks?"

"I mean I don't want to go with you. Would you mind moving now? I'm wanted on stage."

Suzanne no longer wanted to giggle; poor James looked quite dejected. "She fancies Steven," she explained to him in a whisper.

"Yes, well I fancy Becky, but there's no point going for the impossible," he retorted, stalking off.

This time Suzanne laughed aloud at the thought of the pair of them making do with second best.

"Quiet now!" shouted Mike. "Let's have a straight run-through of the second scene. You can have scripts the first time, and then we'll do it again without." The cast groaned.

Steven, James, Suzanne, Becky and Richard were all in the second scene and as usual once the scenery started going up it became more real and so more nerve-racking for them. Added to which, none of them could forget the sight of the dead cat on stage the previous day, so tension was running high. Richard tried to ease the atmosphere by clowning around until Mike stopped him pretty sharply. Then the hall lights dimmed and they began.

Steven actually preferred it once they didn't have scripts to handle. It always made movement difficult, and when he heard Becky deliver his cue line and started to move across towards her he suddenly found that she wasn't in the right place. This threw him. He didn't know if it was Becky's fault or his, but he was left stranded on the wrong side of the stage, having to shout his next lines across at Richard.

Trying to correct the mistake, Richard began to move towards Steven while speaking. Steven watched him, grateful for his help, and then suddenly out of the corner of his eye he saw one of the huge flats start to wobble. For the briefest of moments it trembled as though in a breeze and then, as Steven gave a shout of horror, the top began to slant towards the stage until, with a terrible groaning noise, the entire structure over-balanced and crashed face down onto the stage.

In the few brief seconds that the incident took to happen, they all ran for their lives. They bumped into each other, screamed, pushed and tried frantically to get out of the way. Then, as the whole stage shook beneath the shock of the crushing weight, they stood in the wings, their eyes huge in their pale faces as they checked to see they'd all got safely clear. They hadn't. Beneath the huge white flat one of the group now lay hidden from view, silenced for ever.

Mike was already among them, closely followed by Christine. "Is everyone all right? I couldn't see from where I was sitting. Was anyone hurt?"

It was Steven who spoke. His voice shook but he managed to get the words out. "I can't see Richard anywhere."

Someone gasped with shock. Mike turned to Christine. "Go and ring for an ambulance. Steven, would you, James and Stuart help me lift the flat at once. The rest of you go backstage and stay there until we tell you to come out."

Suzanne cast a fearful look at her brother, then she went off with the rest of the girls while the boys and Mike did what had to be done.

It was nearly an hour before they were told officially that Richard was dead, his skull crushed by the impact. It was Mike who broke the news to them, and then they all had to wait because a policeman and policewoman had to talk to them before they could go home.

"It might have been me!" wailed Becky. "I was standing just in front of him when it began to fall!"

"Do shut up," said Claire sharply. "It might have been any of us, but it was Richard and it's Richard and his family you should be thinking about, not yourself for a change."

This had the effect of making Becky sob all the louder, and she was still sobbing – although without ruining her make-up – when the police arrived.

Their questions were brief and fairly routine. They wanted to know where everyone had been standing when the flat started to fall, both those who were on stage and those who were off. Then they wanted to know if anyone had seen Richard trip, or if he would have been hit anyway, and finally they went over the way the flats had been put up that morning and said they'd probably need to ask more detailed questions about that at another time.

"First the cat and now this!" sobbed Becky.

The policeman, a young and rather attractive sergeant, immediately looked alert. "We haven't heard anything about a cat."

The other girls glared at Becky. Trust her to push herself forward when poor Richard was dead, thought Suzanne, trying not to cry at the thought that she'd never see him clowning around again.

Becky immediately launched into a detailed description of the incident the day before, and the policewoman wrote it all down in her notebook. "Not a very nice thing to happen," said the sergeant sympathetically, "but hardly likely to be connected. This seems a pretty straightforward case of an accident. The affair with the cat was obviously a nasty joke."

Much later that evening, Suzanne told Steven and Stuart what Becky had told the sergeant. "Trust her to talk about herself at a time like that," she said indignantly. "As though you can compare the two incidents at all."

Steven wasn't so sure. "I hope you're right," he said softly, "but you must admit that Becky *was* in front of the flat when it began to fall and whatever the final verdict I just can't believe Mike and the backstage team failed to secure that flat properly."

Suzanne's eyes widened in horror. "You don't honestly think someone made it fall on purpose?"

"I hope not, but coming on top of the cat thing it's a bit worrying," said Steven.

"No one would want to kill Richard!" exclaimed Stuart. "He was just a laugh."

Suzanne, remembering Claire's response to Richard's attempts at amusing her, kept silent.

3

Rehearsals for Christine's play stopped until after the inquest into Richard's death. The group met, but only at their houses, and then all they talked about were the two incidents.

Claire was anxious about their future. Unknown to the group, she relied on her time with them to keep her sane as she coped with an increasingly difficult home situation. "Surely they won't make us close down," she said to Steven as they all gathered in his room one Friday evening. "I'm sure I saw Richard slip. If he hadn't fallen no one would have been hurt."

Suzanne wondered why Claire had never mentioned Richard slipping before. She glanced at Emma, who raised her eyebrows in equal surprise.

"If the *flat* hadn't fallen no one would have been hurt is the point," said Steven shortly. "You know what it's like when something like this happens. They look for someone to blame, and in this case they'll blame the supervision of the set construction, and that will be it for the group."

Claire scowled. "Well, I don't think it's fair."

"I don't care if it does close down," said Becky. "You all seem to forget what happened to me. It was disgusting, and I don't know that I want to belong any more, even if the group keeps going."

"Come on Becky, you don't mean that," said Suzanne.

"Of course she doesn't," sneered Claire. "Where else would she get the chance to play queen bee all the time? Most drama groups want their leading players to be able to act."

"Do shut up!" said Emma sharply. "Richard's dead, that's what matters."

"It's awful at art college now," said James quietly. "They've taken all his work down, as though he never existed, and I have to work alongside someone I've never even met before and who can't paint to save his life. Richard had real talent."

"What do you think, Emma?" asked Steven suddenly. "Will the group survive?" He valued her opinion because she always seemed less emotional than the others in the group.

"I think it will if we fight hard enough for it.

We all know how careful Mike and Christine are, and everything was double-checked that morning. Suzanne and I were there, we've talked it over and remember seeing that for ourselves. I think we ought to be allowed to go up on the stand and say so. Of course it's dreadful that Richard's dead, but people get killed all the time, playing sport, driving cars, crossing roads. It's horrid but it happens. It's up to us to make sure the group isn't closed down."

Steven took hold of her hand, which was resting next to his on the table and she felt a tremor run through her. "Em's right: we have to make sure the coroner hears for himself that the group's properly run."

Emma welcomed the warmth of Steven's fingers round hers and hoped that before too long he would stop seeing her as a kind of second sister and ask her out to the cinema or a party without Suzanne making up their usual threesome.

In the end, they had very little chance to make their voices heard at the inquest. The police sergeant who'd spoken to them all gave his evidence. He made it clear that he believed the wrong knots had been used to secure the flat that fell.

Mike and Christine both had a chance to speak and assured the coroner that they'd checked the knots themselves, separately, and they were the right ones – and totally secure. Then Suzanne was called to say that she had seen them do this. Apart from that, all the evidence was medical and highly unpleasant to hear.

As Steven had feared, the coroner brought in a verdict of accidental death and went on to stress the importance of strict adult supervision at all times when young people were involved in group projects.

A journalist from the local paper came round, talked to all the members, and gave Mike and Christine plenty of space to repeat their assurances that every possible safety precaution was always taken. However, they had to admit that they had absolutely no explanation for what had happened.

All the members told the reporter how much the drama group meant to them, and Stuart and James said that projects like this helped teach you to become part of a team.

"The last thing Richard would have wanted was for the drama group to be closed because of what happened," James added.

In the end it was the intervention of Richard's parents that saved them all. They agreed with what James had said and told the local paper that their son had enjoyed the drama group more than any other activity he'd ever done. "We want to go and see the play that Richard had told us so much about," they said.

*   *   *

Two days later Mike rang Steven to say that the play would be going ahead. "I'm not sure everyone will come back," he said cautiously, "but we'll just have to hope for the best."

He needn't have worried. They all turned up the following Sunday afternoon, including Becky. Claire laughed unpleasantly when she saw her. "What did I tell you?" she said loudly to Suzanne.

Suzanne, who was feeling horribly on edge anyway, turned on Claire. "Don't you ever give up?" she demanded. "No one suits you. Becky's too pretty, Richard was too silly. You're quite difficult to please."

Claire looked startled. "I didn't dislike Richard."

"Yes you did," said Emma. "You said he drove you up the wall."

"He just got on my nerves," protested Claire.

"Well, he won't any more, will he?" Emma pointed out cruelly.

For a moment Claire stared at her in silence then she turned away. "I'm going to go over my lines. If I want to be picked on I can always stay at home."

"What does she mean by that?" asked Emma.

"She's got stepfather trouble at home, or so Christine told me."

"I'll swop her stepfather for my stepsister then," said Emma darkly.

Suzanne gave a sympathetic sigh. "I know Paula's a pain, but she's only five."

"Believe me, a five-year-old has a lot of power, especially a pretty one with a loud voice. I'm surprised our neighbours haven't put their house on the market."

"Look, if I were you I'd . . ."

"Well, you're not, are you?" said Emma shortly. "Can we change the subject? I see Stuart's still besotted with you. He can't stop staring."

Suzanne went pink. "Oh well, perhaps he's okay really – Steven thinks I should go out with him, but I'm not sure."

"Hey, that would be great," said Emma. "Perhaps you could persuade Steven to make a foursome?"

The question hung, unanswered, in the air and Suzanne was relieved when Mike called for silence because she hated to keep disappointing her friend over Steven.

The rehearsal that day was subdued, but Mike didn't criticize anyone. He knew that they had to ease their way back into things and it would take some time before they could relax with the scenery. Several of the girls were particularly nervous of the large backdrops and kept glancing at them as they walked around the stage.

"What can I do to put them at ease?" Mike asked Christine at the end of the afternoon.

Christine linked her arm through his. "Nothing at all, Mike. We just have to be patient."

He nodded. "I kept expecting to see Richard

today. You know how he was always clowning around in the wings, making people giggle and irritating me to hell? Well, today I'd have given everything I owned to have him there again. If it's like that for me, what must it be like for his friends and his family?"

"I know," said Christine. "It makes you wonder why such awful things happen. Everyone feels terrible, and we'd all give anything to have him back. I suppose you just have to keep going."

Mike looked down at her. "Why *did* Richard die? You and I both know the flats were secure. What on earth happened?"

A prickle of fear ran up the back of Christine's neck. "I don't know," she confessed. "I only wish I did."

After a couple of weeks the group was nearly back to normal. Everyone had learned their lines and the play was really beginning to come to life. It was to be put on during the last week of November, which meant they had six weeks left to perfect it. Due to school and college commitments, rehearsals were limited to a couple of evenings a week for those who could make it, and Saturday and Sunday afternoons for everyone. It was rare for anyone to manage both weekend rehearsals, so the number of times when the whole cast was assembled were few, which made life very difficult for Mike.

Luckily, this particular Sunday afternoon was one of those rare occasions and it was decided to run right through the play first, to enable Mike to see exactly where the weaknesses were, and then work on those at times when the people involved were free.

"Keep the pace up; that way we might even get through it twice," he shouted as Christine switched on the stage lights.

"I'll die of hunger," muttered Hazel, standing in the wings.

Emma smiled at her. "You can have some of my sandwiches. I can't eat when I'm acting."

Hazel was so surprised by the smile that she forgot to pick up the prompt book and Lynne had to push it into her hands after Suzanne had fluffed on an opening line.

"Do we have a prompt?" called Mike sarcastically from out front.

"Sorry!" muttered a mortified Hazel, and from then on she concentrated so hard that once or twice she began to prompt when the cast were only pausing for effect.

"You ruined my speech with your stupid prompt!" snapped Claire, coming off-stage from her big scene. "Can't you mark the damned book with 'PAUSE' or something? Honestly!"

By the end of the afternoon they'd gone right through the play twice and at last it was coming together. The same couldn't be said for the cast, who when not on stage were unusually ill at ease with each other.

"This is all wrong," Steven said to Claire as they waited in the wings. "It seems mechnical, totally unreal."

Claire knew what he meant. "We all miss Richard," she said slowly. "At least, I guess that's the problem. I mean, even *I* miss him and he drove me mad, so it must be worse for his close friends, like James."

"Let's go to the pub when we finish," said Steven. "We can talk it over there."

They slipped away quickly, as soon as Mike called a halt.

Suzanne asked Stuart where her brother was.

"No idea," he replied.

"Oh," said Suzanne. "I suppose Emma and I will have to go home without him."

Stuart looked at her a bit nervously. "Are you in any rush? We could go to the bowling alley if you want and have a coke and a chat before going on home."

Suzanne nodded. "Sounds great. Shall I ask Emma too?"

"Erm, not exactly," mumbled Stuart. "I thought it might be nice if it was just the two of us."

"Oh," Suzanne flushed. "Yes, of course. I'll just go and tell Emma."

Emma was waiting by the double doors. "Ready?"

"Er, no, actually I'm not coming home," Suzanne blurted out in a rush. "Stuart's asked me to go to the bowling alley. I'll see you tomorrow at school, if that's okay."

"You'll have to tell me all about it," grinned Emma broadly. "Where's Steven? I'll walk home with him."

"I think he's already gone home to revise," called Suzanne as she hurried away.

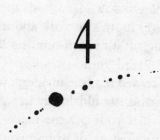

4

The pub was pretty full when Claire and Steven got there. Always a popular meeting place at weekends, it was packed out by nine o'clock.

"Try and find a couple of seats in a corner," suggested Steven. "I'll get the drinks. What would you like?"

"Lager will be fine for me," said Claire, pushing her way through the chattering throng. Spotting a couple about to leave, she pushed even harder and grabbed their seats.

It was a good five minutes before Steven returned. Claire spent the time looking around to see if there was anyone there she knew. She hoped there would be. Most girls fancied Steven. He was tall, fair-haired and well built, and unlike a lot of guys he could talk about other things apart from sport and drinking.

"Sorry I was so long," apologized Steven, when he got back. "They're short-handed behind the bar."

"Doesn't matter. I'm in no rush to get home, I can tell you. My mum's at work and my stepfather will be sleeping off his lunch-time session."

Steven had heard rumours about Claire's stepfather, but he sensed that she wouldn't want obvious sympathy. Neither would he in her place. It was bad enough when your parents made life difficult, without the humiliation of having your friends feel sorry for you as well, so he just nodded.

"The rehearsal was pretty grim wasn't it?" he commented.

"Hideous. I could have screamed when Hazel kept prompting me. I know she's never brilliant, but today she seemed worse than ever."

"Nerves, probably. Did you see the way Emma and Suzanne kept glancing at the flats? They were obviously terrified that one of them was going to fall again."

"Becky wasn't bothered," remarked Claire thoughtfully. "She moaned on about how terrified she was before we began, but once she got on the stage she was all right."

"Probably because she hasn't got much imagination," suggested Steven.

"Everyone else was nervous in one way or another though," commented Claire.

"Well, of course they were. It was the first rehearsal since Richard died," responded Steven, thinking how much more attractive Claire was when she relaxed and stopped being sharp-tongued.

"If someone deliberately unfastened one of those flats then that person wouldn't have been nervous," Claire pointed out. "I thought I'd try and see if I could spot anyone who didn't seem affected, but I couldn't."

"Then maybe it was an accident."

"The cat wasn't an accident," Claire reminded him. "No way could that dead cat have got into the box by mistake. Ugh! When I think that I was holding the box it makes me shudder."

Steven leant across the table towards her. "So you're saying that the two things are connected, which means that Richard was killed on purpose?"

"I don't see how anyone can think anything else."

"But the dead cat didn't hurt anyone. It wasn't going to kill Becky, was it? A falling flat's a different thing altogether."

Claire lowered her voice. "Suppose they're connected, but not necessarily done by the same person?"

Steven stared at her. "What do you mean?"

"I've been thinking about this a lot, and I reckon it could have happened like this: you know what a joker Richard was, the way he liked to play the fool all the time?" Steven nodded. "Well, suppose he put the dead cat in the box as a trick. Maybe he wanted to liven Becky's performance up for us all! Anyway, if that's what happened, isn't it possible that Becky might have guessed it was him once she'd got over the shock?"

"I know you girls don't like Becky much, but the boys do," protested Steven, missing the fleeting look of irritation that crossed Claire's face. "I can't see Richard doing that to her."

"Okay, perhaps he didn't, but suppose Becky thought he did. If anyone had pulled that kind of trick on me, I'd have thought of Richard immediately."

"That's because you didn't like him!" exclaimed Steven.

Claire sighed. "No it isn't. It's because he's the only person in the group who would have considered doing something like that funny. He never thought anything through. He wouldn't have imagined how Becky might have felt, or quite how nasty it would turn out to be, he'd have just thought it was a laugh. Admit it, Steven, Richard wasn't highly sensitive to other people's feelings."

"He was a natural clown, that's all," protested Steven.

Claire wished that just sometimes the boys wouldn't stick up for each other automatically, as though being honest was disloyal or something stupid. "He was a prat, Steven, and you know it," she said shortly.

"He's dead!" exclaimed Steven.

Claire softened her voice. "Do you think I don't know that? It's horrible, and so was his funeral and watching all his family walking behind the coffin, but that doesn't change anything. I'm not saying he was malicious or unkind, but he could be a fool."

Steven spread his hands in resignation. "Okay, I give you that. Sometimes he did fool about too much."

"Right, then we're agreed on that at least, are we?"

Steven nodded, swallowed some of his drink and wondered where the conversation was leading.

"Given that it's certainly possible Becky might have *thought* Richard had played the dead cat trick on her, I think it's more than possible she could have decided to get her revenge on him," Claire continued.

"Revenge?"

"Yes! I think that it might have been Becky who loosened the supporting ropes of the flats. She never usually does much backstage work; she probably didn't even realize how disastrous the outcome would be, but I think she wanted to scare Richard like he'd scared her, by making the scenery wobble. It's just that, being Becky, she didn't know what she was doing and instead of wobbling, it fell."

"But Becky almost got hit," protested Steven. "You know yourself that she was standing near the same flat."

"Standing *near* it, yes, but not so near that she even got grazed by it. Besides, if she'd known what was going to happen, that it was going to wobble and give Richard a scare, then being near would have been her alibi. No one would have suspected her."

"So who were they meant to suspect?" asked Steven curiously.

Claire shrugged. "Knowing Becky, she wouldn't have bothered about that. After all, if Richard was only to have a nasty fright, suspects weren't that important, were they?"

"Is that honestly what you believe happened?" asked Steven.

Claire nodded. "What other explanation is there?"

Steven drained his glass but saw that Claire had hardly started her drink. "I've been thinking that the same person was responsible for both incidents. That's why it's so scary. Everyone else is probably thinking like that too."

"Who?" asked Claire. "I mean, you must have a suspect. I'd really like to know which of us you think is capable of doing both things, and why."

"I'll just get myself another drink, then I'll tell

you," promised Steven.

While he was away, Claire noticed three girls from her college standing at the far end of the room and looking her way. Normally they didn't take much notice of her, but tonight they smiled and waved, and she knew it was because she was with Steven. She smiled to herself. Tomorrow the news would be all round the college that she and Steven were going out together. No one would know that they'd been discussing the drama group's problems all the time. They'd imagine that they were sitting with their heads close together because their talk was so intimate, and she felt a small glow of pleasure. It wasn't often that she had that kind of luck and although she knew that it shouldn't matter what the other girls at college thought of her, it did, far more than she ever let on. She didn't like being alone, and but for her stepfather would have asked friends back home and had a more normal social life. Being out with Steven, for any reason, was giving her a good feeling. Having witnesses was even better.

"There, I was quicker that time," he announced, breaking into her train of thought. "Now, where were we?"

Claire moved so that their heads nearly touched across the small table. "You were going to tell me who you thought was behind the two incidents," she said quietly.

"Well, I haven't managed to come up with a name," admitted Steven. "It did cross my mind that Richard might have stage-managed the cat business, but once he was killed I just decided I'd been wrong and tried to come up with someone who'd been in a position to do both things. That had to mean someone who did backstage work."

"Not an actor, you mean?" asked Claire.

"Well, Stuart and James do both, but Richard was James's closest friend and he's so shattered by what's happened that it can't have been him, and obviously it isn't Stuart, so . . ."

"Why obviously?" asked Claire sharply.

Steven stared at her. "He's my mate. I just know it isn't him."

"That doesn't mean a thing," said Claire. "Remember that book about the Yorkshire Ripper – *Somebody's Husband, Somebody's Son*? Well, this is the same thing. If you're right, then whoever the person is, they've got friends and a family. No one in our group's an outcast. Killers don't wear badges saying, 'I am a psychopath', you know. That's why they often get away with murder."

Steven flushed. "You may be right, but it isn't Stuart," he repeated stubbornly.

Claire sighed. "So much for an unbiased discussion."

"I don't think your theory is exactly unbiased. Everyone knows how much you girls resent Becky getting the part of the daughter in this play. If she were more popular you might have thought twice about putting the blame for Richard's death on her."

Claire got up, grabbing her bag off the table. "I think I'd better go. I'm late home as it is."

Steven stood up too, reaching out a hand to stop her. "Claire, don't rush off, please! I was only pointing out that neither of us can be totally without prejudice."

Claire shook his hand off and made for the door. Steven caught up with her in the car park outside. "Claire, stop! Let me walk you home. You can't . . ."

"I'm not scared of the dark," she said. "Thanks for the drink."

Steven ran to catch up with her. "I'm sorry if I upset you, but Stuart and I have been mates for years."

"I wouldn't know what that's like. I've never been in one place long enough to make friends like that," she admitted, softening a little at his obvious distress.

"I didn't want us to come here only to talk about the group," Steven continued as they walked along the footpath towards where Claire lived. "I wanted to get to know you better. We have so little time when we're rehearsing and . . ."

"There isn't much to know," replied Claire, then

wished she hadn't said that as Steven fell silent. "God, what a mess," she said at last. "We come out for a drink and end up quarrelling. I'm really good at screwing things up."

Steven slipped an arm round her waist. "It was my fault too. I just didn't expect to hear you mention Stuart, but you were right: if there *is* one single person behind the two incidents then it could just as easily be Stuart as anyone else."

"*If* it was, then yes, it could be, but I'm sure my theory's the right one and it's a case of two people playing separate tricks on each other, but one trick went horribly wrong."

"Then how come Becky isn't more upset?" asked Steven curiously, slowing down as they approached Claire's house.

"Perhaps she's just blocked it out of her mind. I think I would if it happened to me. Or maybe, since – in my biased opinion – Becky's thoroughly self-centred, she believes that it isn't her fault. If Richard hadn't been horrid to her she wouldn't have been horrid to him and there you are, total justification."

"For murder?"

Claire felt Steven's fingers tighten round her waist and a thrill of excitement went through her. He really did like her. Ever since she'd first seen him act she'd liked him. Often, when she'd shut herself away in her bedroom to escape the rows at home, she'd pictured herself going out with him, but she hadn't expected it ever to happen. Yet now it was, and all because of Richard's ghastly death.

"No, not for murder," she managed to reply, despite the tightness in her chest and the sudden strange feeling that her lungs wouldn't let her breathe properly any more. "I don't think Becky would ever see it as murder."

"If you're right," said Steven slowly, "then there's no need for everyone to feel on edge during rehearsals, is there?"

"No, because it's over."

"Yet even you were nervous today. You admitted it all felt wrong at the rehearsal."

Claire turned to face him, and Steven pulled her towards him so that their bodies were almost touching. "That's true," she admitted, feeling her heart racing and hoping he didn't realize how much he was affecting her, because she wanted to seem the same cool Claire as usual. "I don't know why that was. Probably everyone else's uneasiness rubbed off on me. I didn't feel threatened exactly, just weird. No one was behaving naturally and it was more like a dream than the real thing."

Steven agreed. "That's exactly right. Look, Claire, I don't know if I can go along with your theory but that doesn't matter, does it? I mean . . ." He hesitated and Claire looked steadily at him. "We could go out together again, couldn't we?"

"Sure."

"Perhaps to the cinema?" suggested Steven, his own heart pounding with relief that he'd managed to avoid the quarrel that had threatened. "There's the latest Keanu Reeves film on next week. You like him, don't you?"

"How did you know that?" asked Claire curiously.

"I heard you telling Suzanne! Shall we go then?"

"Okay. Friday's a good night for me." She glanced over her shoulder, saw a shape at the front window of her home and pulled away from Steven's grasp. "See you at the next rehearsal then. Thanks again for the drink."

Steven watched her walk away from him, and knew that he definitely wanted to get to know her better. She was quite different from any other girl he'd been out with, far more reserved, and he found that intriguing.

At the same time as Steven and Claire were talking in the pub, Stuart and Suzanne were doing the same thing at the recently opened ten-pin bowling alley at the opposite end of the town.

Stuart was so pleased to have prised Suzanne away from Emma, that he couldn't think of a thing to say once he'd bought them both cokes. For what seemed endless minutes they sat drinking them in total silence, watching those who were playing.

"Have you ever played?" Suzanne asked at last, afraid the silence would go on the whole evening.

"Only once; it's a bit expensive for me. Besides, I'm not very good."

"Nor am I. A group of us came here for Emma's birthday and most of my balls went down the gully. I broke a fingernail as well, so I don't think I'll bother again."

"You and Emma are really close, aren't you?"

"No closer than you and Steven," retorted Suzanne.

"It's different with girls. You seem to sort of shut other people out. I wanted to ask you to Richard's birthday party last year but I didn't because I was sure you'd say no."

"Why? I said yes this time, didn't I?"

"That's different. Loads of people went to Richard's party, but Emma wasn't one of them and I thought you wouldn't go unless she was asked too."

Suzanne swivelled round on her stool. "I suppose I might not have done. She'd have felt left out."

"Doesn't she ever go anywhere without you?"

"Yes, sometimes, but that's different. Emma's got problems at home; she's easily hurt."

"So, what about Richard then?" Stuart asked, abruptly changing the subject. "I mean, do you think his death was an accident or what?"

Suzanne shook her head. "I don't see how it

could have been. Emma and I saw those flats being put up, and watched Mike and Christine check the knots. It couldn't have been an accident."

"I don't think it was either, and nor does James."

"Who do you think did it then?" asked Suzanne softly.

"I've no idea. It isn't possible to think of any of us killing Richard, is it? Why should they? It isn't as though he was taking anyone's favourite part or anything like that. He was just a laugh, someone who liked to have a good time."

"His idea of a good time wasn't the same as everyone else's," Suzanne pointed out.

"I guess not, but what I was trying to say was that when Becky was given that dead cat it could have been any of you girls who'd decided to take revenge on her, for getting the part she did, only with Richard there was no motive."

Suzanne felt herself flushing. "Are you saying that it was one of us girls who put the dead cat in the box?"

Stuart looked uncomfortable. "I suppose I am."

"What a cheek! It's more like the kind of silly joke Richard would have played."

"Maybe, but he wouldn't have killed himself as a follow-up, would he?"

Suzanne slumped on her stool. "No, he wouldn't. That doesn't mean it was a girl though. Perhaps

Becky turned down one of you boys. You all drool over her enough; maybe one of you was fed up because she wouldn't go out with you and used the dead cat to punish her."

Stuart had to admit Suzanne had a point. "Suppose that's true, why go on to kill Richard?"

"That's the problem, isn't it? There's no connection between the two of them that springs to mind. I think that's why everyone was so nervous at rehearsal today. We were all wondering which one of us might be next."

"There is one connection," said Stuart slowly. "Claire didn't like either of them."

"Claire?"

"Yeah. She hated Becky for getting that part, and she didn't find Richard's antics at all funny. If you remember she didn't laugh at his cartoon of her as a leopard, and then she really gave him a look when he was playing the fool in the wings during one of the acts."

"You think she killed him for playing the fool?" asked Suzanne incredulously.

"Sshh! No, not necessarily. I'm only saying she *might* have done. That if you look for any connection, however slight, between the two incidents, Claire is the only one that comes up."

"I know she's a bit aloof," said Suzanne, "but that doesn't mean she's a killer. If Claire could do it, then so could any of us. We're all the same, at least on the surface. I don't see why you've picked on her. Why not me?"

For a moment they stared at each other. Stuart knew that he liked Suzanne; he'd wanted to ask her out for ages. Now he'd done it and she'd accepted, but what she was saying was true and if he was honest he had to admit that it was just as possible for Suzanne to have killed Richard as Claire, except that he couldn't believe her capable of it.

Suzanne was looking at Stuart and thinking almost exactly the same thing. She knew now that she liked him, and she'd liked him for some time without admitting it to herself, but suppose *he* was Richard's murderer? How could she start suddenly trusting him with all her thoughts and feelings when he might be the person who'd stood behind the flats and slowly untied the knots, replacing them with something far less secure? He often helped out backstage; it wouldn't have been impossible for him to do it. She didn't believe that he had, but it was possible.

"Why did all this have to happen?" she exclaimed miserably. "It gets in the way of everything."

Stuart reached for her hand. "It won't go on for ever. If someone did kill Richard they'll be caught in the end, and then things will go back to how they were before."

"But they won't. Emma and I were talking about that, and she said that even when we find out who the murderer is, the group won't be the same because one of us will have turned out to be quite different from what we believed, so how can we ever trust anyone again?"

"I suppose you just do," said Stuart helplessly. "It isn't the kind of thing you know about until it happens, is it? I mean, there isn't any group you can contact that helps you deal with having a killer in your midst."

"Don't!" exclaimed Suzanne. She finished her coke. "I'd better be going."

"I'll walk you back. Suzie, I don't suppose you'll believe me but I've still got to say it, I didn't kill Richard, nor did I put that dead cat in the box for Becky."

"Neither did I," said Suzanne.

They smiled tentatively at each other, and held hands all the way home, yet there was still a barrier between them because they were both intelligent enough to know that no matter how they felt about each other, Richard's murder was going to affect all relationships until the killer's identity was discovered.

"So, you don't think it was Claire?" asked Stuart as they stood at Suzanne's front gate.

"No more than I think it was anyone else, no."

"You don't think it's more likely to be her than, say, your brother?"

Suzanne snatched her hand away from his.

"That's a foul thing to say."

"Why? You said it was no more likely to be her than anyone else in the group."

"That's right, and I meant it too. It could just as well have been Steven, or Emma, or you come to that," she shouted. "We have no idea, have we?"

Stuart turned away, knowing that he'd made an utter mess of their first time out together. "I still think Claire's the most likely suspect," he said stubbornly.

"Just because she didn't fall about laughing at Richard's jokes it doesn't make her a murderer," Suzanne said crossly, but she felt utterly miserable as she went indoors. It was a rotten way to end the evening.

5

Because Suzanne had gone off with Stuart, and Steven was nowhere in sight, Emma ended up walking home with Hazel and Lynne who lived nearby. After all the stress of the rehearsal, it was a disappointing way to end the day.

"I didn't enjoy this afternoon much," muttered Hazel. "Everyone was so snappy."

Emma glanced at Hazel's downcast face. "You mean Claire was snappy, as usual. I wouldn't let her bother you. She's got an attitude problem if you ask me."

"It wasn't only Claire," remarked Lynne. "I thought we were all pretty wound up, but after what happened to Richard, that's not surprising. I'm glad I'm not on stage. Didn't you wonder if something was going to happen to you, Emma?"

Emma, fed up that Suzanne had gone off and left her, was kicking at a discarded crisp packet and didn't seem to hear.

"Emma!"

She jumped. "Sorry, what was that?"

"I said weren't you frightened of something happening to you today?" repeated Lynne, wondering what had been occupying Emma's mind.

"No."

"You hurried past the flat that fell on Richard pretty quickly," said Hazel. "I could see you from the prompt corner."

"I did not! Why should I worry? Who'd want to kill me?"

"Who'd want to kill Richard?" asked Lynne. "I think it must have been a freak accident. Or maybe someone thought they tightened those knots but really they loosened them, only now they don't like to own up."

"You can't loosen knots by mistake!" said Emma scathingly. "Once Mike had checked them we all knew they weren't allowed to be touched, which means that if anyone did go near them it was because they wanted to cause trouble."

"I suppose Mike might have made a mistake," said Hazel doubtfully.

"Not Christine as well though, and Suzanne and

I saw the pair of them checking the flats were secure," responded Emma.

"Well, after what happened to Becky I think it's spooky," said Lynne. "Maybe the stage is haunted," she added in a rush. "You know, like in 'Phantom of the Opera.'"

Emma looked at her in disbelief. "You're pathetic, Lynne! What sort of ghost would there be in a community hall in Dorking?"

"It's possible. My mum believes in ghosts. She says . . ."

"I doubt if Richard's parents do," Emma pointed out cuttingly.

Hazel tried to calm things down. "Lynne was only trying to come up with an answer. Okay, so a ghost is out of the question but someone played that trick on Becky and now Richard's dead. Don't you think it's as though we're cursed? I mean, is trouble going to keep following us around?"

Lynne shivered. "If it is, I'll leave. Richard could be a pain but it's weird without him. Even though he isn't there I keep forgetting he's dead and we won't ever see him again. It's so horribly final."

"Death *is*," Emma pointed out.

"I do amateur dramatics for fun, not to be scared out of my wits," Lynne retorted. "I hope nothing else happens."

Hazel looked horrified. "You don't think anything else *will* happen, do you, Lynne? Em?"

Emma stopped walking and stared at her. "How should we know?"

Hazel went pink. "I didn't mean . . . I just hoped you might have worked out . . ."

"Well, I for one haven't worked anything out and I've no idea what else will happen." Emma's body was stiff with tension.

Hazel smiled tentatively. "I didn't mean anything, Emma. It came out wrong, that's all."

Emma suddenly relaxed. "It's all right. I know you didn't. I'm just in a foul mood tonight anyway."

"Has Suzanne gone out with Stuart?" asked Lynne as they approached the end of the road where she and Hazel lived.

"I'm not in a foul mood because she's gone out with Stuart, I'm fed up because I've got to look after Paula tonight."

"I saw Suzanne and Stuart leave together," confirmed Hazel. "James wants to take you out, Em. Do you like him?"

"He's all right, but only as a friend. It's Steven I want to go out with," confided Emma.

"Oh, but he's . . ." Lynne broke off as Hazel kicked her unobtrusively on the ankle.

"He's what?" demanded Emma.

"Always busy," finished Lynne weakly. "What with his studying and acting, and then he plays loads of sport, or so my brother tells me. He says

Steven would be unbearable if he weren't so useless at anything mechanical or electrical. No good marrying him if you want a man to change your fuse boxes, Emma!"

Hazel and Lynne began to giggle and Emma walked away from them. "See you at the next rehearsal," she called.

The other two watched her go. "Why did you kick me?" asked Lynne.

"Because you were about to say he'd taken Claire out tonight, weren't you?"

"Yes."

"Well, Emma won't want to know. She's obsessed with Steven – has been for the past year. If you ask me, that's why she's so thick with Suzanne, and I don't want to see her hurt."

"She'll have to find out some time."

"Not from us," said Hazel firmly. "Emma's always nice to me and I don't want to be around when she does find out. Anyway, Steven and Claire might not be an item for long and then she would have been hurt for nothing."

"I think you're being stupid," said Lynne. "We'd all like to go out with Steven, but there are plenty of other blokes who are neat too."

As Emma left the other two girls behind, her footsteps began to slow. She was thinking about Suzanne's face when she'd asked her if Steven had left the rehearsal hall. Although Suzanne had said her brother had hurried away to do some revision, there'd been a hesitation before she spoke, an almost guilty look in her eyes, and Emma had the nasty feeling her friend wasn't telling the truth.

She could think of only one reason why Suzanne would lie to her, and that would be because Steven had already left with a girl from the group and she didn't want Emma to know.

This seemed the most likely explanation, and Emma could guess who it was as well – Claire. She'd seen the two of them talking earlier, and she'd watched Steven studying Claire when she was on stage. It was plain that he admired her. She felt thoroughly fed up. Claire was sarcastic and no fun at all. Why should she be more attractive to Steven than Emma?

The answer was only too clear. It wasn't her fault, it was because Steven knew her too well. She and Suzanne had been friends for several years and she'd spent a lot of time in their home. She'd suspected for some time that Steven saw her more as a sister than a potential girlfriend, and this confirmed it.

"You're late," said Emma's mother as her daughter walked in the door. "Have you forgotten you're looking after Paula this evening? David and I are going out with Liz and Phil for a drink."

"I know! The rehearsal went on a long time. It

isn't easy working on a play when one of your friends has just been killed on stage, you know," retorted Emma. "Who are Liz and Phil anyway? Friends of *his*, I suppose!"

Her mother's lips tightened. "They're old friends of David, yes."

"How nice that he's widened your social circle for you. It's just a pity he hasn't done the same for mine. I could have gone to the bowling alley with Suzanne and Stuart tonight if I hadn't had to come home to look after Paula," she added untruthfully.

Paula, a fair-haired, plump five-year-old came running into the hallway. "Read me a story!" she demanded, thrusting a book at Emma.

"I haven't taken my coat off yet!" exclaimed Emma irritably. "I'm hungry too. Did you save me any tea, Mum?"

"It's on the breakfast bar. Put it in the micro-wave for five minutes."

"Read to me *now*!" repeated Paula loudly, her bottom lip beginning to tremble.

Emma glared at her, and just then David, her stepfather, came out of the living room.

"Hi, Em! Good rehearsal?"

"I prefer to be called Emma except by my friends," she reminded him icily.

David, a tall, dark-haired, handsome man in his early forties, glanced at her, and at the searching look in his brown eyes she felt a stab of guilt although she didn't know why. "Don't stare at me," she said loudly. "I hate it when you do that."

"I wasn't staring at you," he said softly. "I thought you looked a bit upset, that's all."

"I was fine until I got back here."

"Read!" Paula commanded, tugging at the leg of Emma's jeans.

David scooped his daughter up under one arm. "Leave Emma alone, Paula. She's been busy all afternoon and the last thing she wants is you pestering her. Come on, it's time for your bath."

Paula opened her mouth and began to scream as her father carried her upstairs.

Emma went into the kitchen, shoved her plate into the microwave and tried to imagine her home as it used to be, before her mother re-married. Admittedly they hadn't had much money, and her mother had often been out at work when Emma came in from school or visiting friends, but that had meant she'd had more privacy and when they were together she and her mother had been really close. Now they hardly ever talked about anything that mattered because either Paula was around getting in the way or David was there, and no matter how hard he worked at including Emma in their conversation, she knew that really they would have preferred to be alone together.

The timer went off and she took her plate out. Sitting at the table she began to read her horoscope in the paper, but then her mother came in.

"Are you all right, Emma?"

"Fine," she mumbled, her mouth full of food.

"David thought you looked a little pale."

"Tell him to stop looking at me all the time. It's horrible, I don't like it."

"He doesn't look at you all the time. Surely you'd rather he was interested in you, wouldn't you? I know it's difficult adjusting to all the changes, Emma, but . . ."

"Look Mum, I'm really tired and you want to go out. Can we talk about this some other time?"

Her mother saw the closed look on Emma's face and knew there was no point in trying to go on.

"David's getting Paula into bed. If you could just read her one story before you put her light out it would be a great help. She's so fond of you and . . ."

Emma glared at her mother. "Paula isn't fond of me, she just wants everyone's attention all the time and screams if she doesn't get it. She's spoilt, Mum, and you know it."

"She's only five."

"So, when does it stop? When she's six? Seven? Or will you still be giving in to her when she's my age?"

"Something wrong?" asked David, coming into the room and putting an arm around his wife's shoulder.

Emma felt hot with anger, but she kept her eyes

on her plate. "No, nothing's wrong."

"Good, because if there are things going wrong they should be talked about by all of us."

"Won't you be late?" asked Emma, looking up at the kitchen clock. Her mother gave a little squeal and hurried upstairs to finish getting ready.

David took a seat at the table with Emma, who moved her chair further away. "This has to stop, Emma," he said gently. "It isn't fair taking it out on your mother all the time. I can understand you finding Paula difficult, but you've got to understand that it's all strange for her too. Her own mother died when she was three, and since then she's been with a string of. . ."

"I know all that," said Emma tightly. "I am just tired after rehearsing, and rather upset about Richard's death. It was the first rehearsal without him today and it brought it home to us all."

"Sure, I can understand that."

"Good. Tell Paula I'll read her one story as long as she then shuts up and goes to sleep," added Emma as David left her to finish her meal in peace.

Once her mother and stepfather had gone, she read two of Roald Dahl's Revolting Rhymes to Paula, then shut her door, went downstairs and turned the television up loud so that she couldn't hear her yelling any more. The yelling finally stopped after about half an hour, and then Emma sat watching a film but her mind was elsewhere. She was wondering where Steven was at that moment, and if Claire was with him.

By the time Steven got home from the pub, Suzanne was already back from the bowling alley. Steven went into her room where she was watching a Mel Gibson video.

"What's that?"

She tore her eyes reluctantly away from the screen. "*Forever Young*. It's gorgeous."

"Turn it off, Suzie, will you? I want to talk."

Suzanne reluctantly did as he'd asked. "Did you and Claire have a good time?"

Steven's face lit up. "Yes, we did. I nearly blew it at one stage by disagreeing with her theory about the dead cat and Richard's death, but in the end it was all right. We're going to a Keanu Reeves film next week."

"You loathe Keanu Reeves!"

"Claire likes him."

Suzanne pulled a face. "You must really be keen."

"What's wrong with that?"

She didn't quite know what to say and fiddled with the edge of her duvet. "It's just that at the moment, we don't really know who we can trust, do we? It's common knowledge that Claire and Becky don't get on, plus Claire was probably more irritated by Richard than anyone, so . . ."

"You mean you think *Claire* killed Richard?" demanded Steven.

"No, I mean that Claire could have killed Richard. So could I, or you, or Emma or Stuart."

"Plus everyone backstage," Steven pointed out.

"Yes."

"Then why the emphasis on Claire?"

"There isn't an emphasis on Claire. I was only surprised you were willing to start getting involved with anyone while this is going on."

"I suppose this is Stuart's idea?"

"It was one of his ideas, and you have to admit it makes some kind of sense."

"Yes," said Steven slowly, "I can see why he might think of her, but he's wrong."

"How do you know?" asked Suzanne.

"I just do."

"You can't know unless you have proof someone else did it." Suzanne was surprised at herself. She rarely argued with Steven.

Steven shook his head. "Honestly, Suzie, this isn't like you."

"Stuart and I talked it all over and we agreed that it could be anyone."

"Even you or me?" Steven asked his sister.

Suzanne wouldn't look at him. "I suppose so, but that wasn't what I meant."

"Yes you did. You said it could be anyone, and that includes us."

"All right then," said Suzanne, her voice rising. "Let's say it might be one of us two."

"That's utterly ridiculous!"

"Is it?"

"Why would we do it?"

Suzanne wished they could stop talking about it and she could escape into the Mel Gibson film again. Richard's death had already come between her and Stuart, now it was coming between her and Steven as well. "I've no idea," she admitted. "But then I've no idea why anyone would do anything to harm someone in the group. I thought we were all friends, but obviously I was wrong."

"Claire thinks it was two separate incidents, with different people behind them," said Steven. He didn't want to tell Suzanne all the details, but felt she should know something of what he and Claire had discussed.

"That sounds pretty far-fetched."

"Not the way she put it; there is a connection but . . ."

"It sounds as though Claire's put her mind to this quite a lot," said Suzanne.

"She's worried, like we are, that's all. I know she can be sharp sometimes but underneath she isn't like that," said Steven. "She's really nice, and . . ."

"Okay, I accept you're smitten by her. I'm sure that's very nice for you both."

"I like her, yes. What's wrong with that?" asked

Steven in surprise.

"Nothing," admitted Suzanne. "It's only that Emma's so keen on you I was hoping you might take her out some time."

"Emma?"

"Yes, remember Emma?"

"No need to be sarcastic. I'm sorry, Suzie, but much as I like Emma I don't see her in that way. She's more like a second sister than a girlfriend. After all, she's been friends with you for years. I can remember her when she was about ten."

"Well, she isn't ten now and she hoped you'd take her out."

Steven shook his head. "No chance. I like her a lot, but only as a friend. How did you and Stuart get on, apart from picking on Claire, that is."

"We didn't 'pick on Claire' and we got on fine, thank you. I thought you'd be pleased; you've been on at me enough to go out with him."

"Are you seeing him again?"

"I expect so, but it isn't that easy at the moment. Unlike you, neither Stuart nor I feel we can dismiss anyone out of hand as being Richard's killer, which rather gets in the way of getting to know each other better."

"You can't suspect Stuart!" protested Steven, defending his friend for the second time that evening.

"Wake up, Steven! I can suspect anyone I like.

None of us has any idea who's behind frightening Becky and killing Richard and, until we know the answer, everyone's under suspicion."

"You're absolutely right," said Steven shortly. "I'm pleased you can be so detached and sensible about all this, Suzie, but as far as I'm concerned Claire is definitely in the clear."

"What about me?"

"If I say you're in the clear too then you'll tell me I'm being even more stupid so I don't think I'll answer that one," responded Steven. "Goodnight. Enjoy Mel Gibson."

Suzanne sat on her bed after he'd gone, thinking. It was the first time they'd ever really quarrelled, and she still wasn't quite sure how it had happened. She knew one thing though: Stuart was right. No one could be dismissed as a possible suspect, not even Steven after his outburst this evening; because what did he know about Richard's death that he could be so positive Claire was innocent?

Feeling horribly alone, she started to watch the video again.

6

James Desmond and his parents lived in a three-storey house on the outskirts of Dorking. Both his older brothers were working in London, one as an illustrator of children's books and the other as a graphic designer. The whole family excelled at art. Mrs Desmond was famous locally for her pottery, while Mr Desmond did a strip cartoon for one of the national papers.

As a result, the whole house was like an art gallery. Paintings by various members of the family were hung on the walls, large pieces of pottery cluttered every available surface and all of the carpets and furniture were brightly coloured, but in unusual combinations.

Stuart loved the house, and when he called in on

James the following Saturday morning he thought, as always, how much he would have liked to live in a house like it. His was quite the opposite. His mother spent every minute of the day polishing, hoovering and tidying so that quite often he couldn't find something he'd put down only half an hour earlier. Shoes had to be taken off and left inside the front door the moment anyone stepped inside, and the colour schemes in all the rooms were subdued and perfectly matched.

"I bet you never get moaned at to pick your clothes up!" he exclaimed to James, surveying the chaos in the hall. "If my mother could see this she'd be dashing straight to the cupboard and getting out the black rubbish bags!"

"My mother hates housework, which is great."

"Certainly is," agreed Stuart, following James upstairs to his bedroom. "I always feel relaxed here. At home I daren't sprawl anywhere in case I rumple a cushion!"

"Anyone can relax here anytime. I wish Emma would," James added. "I'd really like to take her out, but she doesn't seem interested."

"She might be now," said Stuart. "The only reason she wasn't before was because she's mad about Steven. Well, I saw him and Claire at the pictures last night. This might be your chance. Give her a ring later and see."

"Saying what?" asked James, leading Stuart

through into the large attic bedroom with its huge skylight window, which gave him good light for his painting. "Hey, Emma, now that Steven's got off with Claire would you like to come out with me? I'm sure she'd be thrilled."

"You'd have to be more subtle than that! Just tell her you'd really like to take her out and get to know her a bit better."

"I'll think about it. Are we going into town this morning?"

"Yeah. I've got to get a pair of jeans. We could have a burger and coke and then go straight on to the rehearsal."

James nodded, but without much enthusiasm.

"Are you out of money?" asked Stuart, who often couldn't make his allowance last the week. "If you are I can get the burgers."

"It isn't that, it's the thought of the rehearsal. I've had a rotten week at art college. I think I'm the only one who misses Richard – everyone else seems to have forgotten all about him. And as for the idiot who works next to me, he hardly knows one end of a paintbrush from the other. The thought of another rehearsal on top of that isn't much fun.

"We saw so much of each other, being at the same college and that. We'd even planned to go to London when we'd finished, try for jobs in the film industry. Suddenly there's this blank space and I've lost my enthusiasm for it all."

Stuart didn't know what to say. "Have you thought about how Richard might have been killed?" he asked at last, but not really expecting a positive answer.

"Yes!" said James excitedly, "I have, and I think I know what happened."

Stuart's eyes widened in surprise. "What?"

"I haven't been sleeping well at night, and while I've been awake I've gone over and over every possibility. Shall I tell you what I think?"

"Of course!"

"I think Becky's behind it all."

Stuart stared at James's excited face and wondered if he'd heard right. "Becky?"

"Yeah."

"But she was the one who got given the dead cat. You were there. You saw the way she reacted. She isn't a good enough actress to have been pretending to be shocked. She was scared stiff."

"I don't think she was. I know she can't act in our plays, but she acts all the time in real life. Think of the way she tosses her hair around and bats her eyelashes at every male within a mile. That's acting, isn't it?"

"I'm not sure," said Stuart doubtfully.

"I am. The way I see it is this. Becky loves the limelight. She knows she isn't popular with the other girls and probably that cat thing was to try and get a bit of sympathy from everyone. It also meant she was centre stage in every way that day. Right, having done that and got sympathy from Mike and everyone else in the group, she decides to take it a bit further. She loosens the knots on a flat that she knows she'll be near, but makes sure she doesn't get right in front of it. When it fell she probably thought everyone would get away but she could make a great fuss about having been the closest to getting hurt. Coming on top of the cat thing she'd certainly have been the focus of attention again. Only it went wrong. Stupid Becky hadn't thought it through and poor Richard got killed."

"I know she likes attention," said Stuart slowly, "but isn't all that a bit extreme? The way she looks she gets plenty of attention anyway."

"Yeah, but not Mike's! I heard her telling some of the girls the other week that she'd do anything to go out with him. She was saying she'd always wanted an older man. I reckon she thought Mike would be forced to pay her more attention, then when he did she'd go to work on him and he'd fall madly in love with her."

"I don't know," said Stuart doubtfully.

"Why not? It all fits."

"Sure, it fits, but the thing is Becky isn't bright enough to think something like that through. She's gorgeous to look at but there isn't much in her head and she'd be too scared of breaking a fingernail to go fiddling with those tight knots."

James's face fell. "But what other explanation is there? I refuse to believe someone deliberately murdered Richard. No one had a motive."

"He could get on some people's nerves a bit," said Stuart cautiously, not wanting to hurt James any more than he'd been hurt already. "Not everyone thought he was funny."

"I know that, but you don't kill someone because they irritate you. And anyway, there's just no connection between Richard and Becky unless you accept that Becky's behind it all."

"Well . . ."

"Have you got a better theory then?" demanded James.

Stuart hesitated. "It's only an idea, and when I mentioned it to Suzanne she was furious."

"Tell me!" said James urgently.

"I thought that it could have been Claire."

"Claire? Why her?"

"She was jealous of Becky, and Richard annoyed her."

James shook his head. "She's far too sensible to go round killing people who irritated her. You know what she's like, she just cuts them down with her tongue."

"I still think she'd be capable of killing," confessed Stuart. "I'd never dare say so to Steven, but there's something strange about her. She's kind of detached from everyone around her, as though she doesn't belong."

"You might just as well choose Emma. She wanted the part Becky got in the last play, and then when Becky received those rave reviews Emma was totally fed up."

"That isn't enough of a motive."

"Not on its own perhaps, but Becky's always giving Steven the eye too, and you know how potty Emma is about him."

"Becky gives every bloke the eye; Emma wouldn't be bothered by that. She'd have more reason to get her own back on Claire than Becky. Besides, why should Emma want to kill Richard?"

"No reason, except for the one you've given Claire, that she got fed up with him messing about all the time. It wouldn't be murder though, not for either of them. More a dangerous stunt that went wrong."

"Then you're not afraid when the group meets?" asked Stuart curiously. "You honestly believe that whoever was behind it all never intended for Richard to die?"

"I've told you what I believe, that Becky was behind both scenes and she certainly won't try anything else after Richard's death so why should I be afraid? No, I'm not paranoid about something happening to me. I just wish Richard was here."

He slumped on the edge of his bed and put his

head in his hands. Stuart didn't agree with his theory and was afraid, but right now James needed help, not another post-mortem. "Let's hit the streets," he said cheerfully. "There's a sale on in the jeans shop; maybe I can find something there I can afford. Remember to bring anything you need for the rehearsal if you're not coming back here."

"So, Claire and Steven are really going out together, are they?" asked James as they left the house.

"Looks that way. Suzanne says Steven's keener than he's ever been on a girl. No accounting for taste. I'd hate to get on the wrong side of her, I can tell you."

At that precise moment, Claire's stepfather was doing just that. Claire had risen early that morning to put three lots of washing in the front-loader, and she'd got it all out on the line before her mother got up. She'd heard Mum come in at three that morning after working the late shift at the factory and knew she'd need to lie-in for a few hours.

However, by nine o'clock her mother was dressed and cooking breakfast for her husband, who hadn't yet put in an appearance. Claire looked at the older woman's white face and realized that she was losing weight.

"Why don't you go back to bed, Mum? I've got

the washing done, and if Martin wants a cooked breakfast let him do it himself. He doesn't work, the least he can do is help around the house a bit even if it's only feeding his own face."

"Don't, Claire," said her mother wearily. "I know how you feel about him but he's my husband and . . ."

"He's lazy, he won't try and find work, he drinks and he hits you," said Claire coldly. "You don't owe him a thing. In fact, you owe it to your-self to chuck him out. You own this house, tell him to go."

"I can't, Claire. We haven't been married for two years yet!"

"You mean there's a set time before you can admit you made a mistake?"

"I've got a headache, Claire. Please don't shout."

Claire sat down opposite her mother. She lowered her voice, filled with compassion for the exhausted figure in front of her, but knowing only too well that she had to be firm because her mother seemed incapable of standing up to her second husband.

"He doesn't care about you; why should you care about him? What's he ever done for you since you got married? Tell me one thing."

"It's hard for him being out of work, Claire. It makes a man feel inadequate."

"Mum, he *is* inadequate, and he'll continue to

be like this as long as you let him. Tell me, where does he get the money that he uses to go drinking?"

"It's his unemployment money."

"And some of your wages, and most of the maintenance Dad pays for me!"

Her mother shook her head. "I know how it looks to you, but . . ."

"Go back to bed. I'll cook his stupid breakfast if it matters that much. You need more rest."

"But there's the shopping to do. We're low on everything."

"Then Martin can take me to the supermarket and I'll go round with the list. At least he can drive."

Worn out by exhaustion and Claire's relentless pressure, her mother finally gave in and went back to bed. It was over an hour before Martin came down, and by then Claire had thrown away what her mother had been cooking and was ironing the first of the dry clothes.

"Where's your mother?" he demanded.

"Sleeping in the spare room. She's tired after the late shift."

"And what am I supposed to eat?"

"There's cereal in the cupboard, and the toaster's on the worktop there. Do you know how to work it?" she added sweetly.

Martin scowled at her. "Your mother knows I like a cooked breakfast."

"Cook it yourself then," snapped Claire, ironing furiously. Martin took a step towards her, and Claire lifted up the steam iron. "Come any closer and I'll iron your face. My mother might let you get violent but I'm not going to."

He stopped and backed away. "You're more trouble than you're worth," he muttered. "The sooner you've finished that secretarial course at college and got yourself a job the better."

"Believe me, I can't wait to get out of here either. Oh yes, and when you've eaten I need a lift to the supermarket. We're out of food."

He stared at her in disbelief. "I'm not going shopping! That's a woman's job."

"I didn't ask you to shop," replied Claire, ironing a crease into one of his shirts with some satisfaction. "All you have to do is drive me there and wait in the car park to bring me home."

"I'm going out at twelve."

"Really? Where could that be to, I wonder?" she asked rudely. "The Bells or the Blue Pig?"

"It's none of your business."

"It *is* my business!" shouted Claire, grabbing at another shirt. "It's my money you're spending."

"You don't have any money; you're still being educated."

"Dad pays money for me."

Martin laughed harshly. "Not enough to compensate for living with you, believe me."

"Don't you care about my mother?" demanded Claire. "Why did you marry her if you were going to treat her like this? She's worn out running round trying to make ends meet."

"Shut up!" he snarled, pouring some cereal into a bowl. "If you want a lift to the supermarket then just shut up, right?"

It was a victory, and they both knew it, so Claire finished the ironing in silence. At last he was going to help out while her mother rested.

As soon as the ironing was done she collected a coat and the housekeeping money then stood waiting in the hall while Martin rang his friends explaining that he'd be late because he was having to do the shopping as his wife was still in bed. Claire didn't care what he told them. It was enough to get him out of the house for a visit to somewhere other than a pub.

Then, just as they were about to leave, her mother came down the stairs. "I can take you, darling," she said to Claire. Her daughter stared at her in disbelief. "It's all right, Martin, you go out with your friends," her mother continued.

"I thought you were worn out," he muttered.

"I was a bit tired, but I've had a doze and I'm fine now."

Claire realized her mother had put make-up on and taken a lot of trouble to look fine, but she was still drawn and there were dark circles beneath her eyes.

Martin flashed a glance of triumph at his step-daughter. "There you are, a fuss about nothing as usual. Don't interfere again, because you don't know as much as you think."

He slammed out of the house and Claire glared at her mother. "How could you? He was going to take me! He had actually given in for once in his selfish life and you had to go and spoil it. Why?"

Her mother put a hand on Claire's shoulder. "It wouldn't have been worth it, darling. I know you meant well and I'm grateful, but I have to live with him. He'd have nursed a grudge about it for the rest of the day and probably all night as well. I couldn't face that."

"You're afraid of him!"

"Claire, it's too easy to make judgements about other people. You don't understand . . ."

"Yes I do. You were afraid he'd take it out on you if I made him drive me to the supermarket. God, how can you stay married to him? I'm never going to get married, never. Men aren't worth it."

"I thought we'd be better off with a man in the house," her mother said as they drove down the high street.

"Well, that goes to show how wrong you can be," replied Claire and they did their shopping in total silence while Claire shook with suppressed rage at her inability to do anything to change their situation.

7

That afternoon, when the group met, Mike introduced Chris, a pupil from the school where he taught drama, who he'd been coaching to take Richard's part.

"Luckily he's got a good memory, so *everyone's* lines should be learnt by next week," he added.

For once the rehearsal went very smoothly and Chris fitted in well. When not actually on stage, the cast were all being measured up for their costumes. The setting was late Victorian and Christine kept telling the girls that they had to look as though they had small waists.

"I don't want to wear something tight," complained Emma. "If I can't breathe properly I feel faint."

"Then try eating fewer cakes for a couple of weeks," snapped Christine.

Emma raised her eyebrows at Suzanne. It was most unlike Christine to lose her temper over anything.

"At least Claire's slim," Christine added, as Claire came in to join them and try on her dress which was the first to be completely finished.

"That's because she burns up all the calories overworking her sharp tongue," quipped Emma.

Claire ignored her and pulled the dress on over her head. "That style really suits you," said Christine approvingly. "It's a pity you weren't . . ." She seemed to change her mind and her voice trailed off.

"A pity I wasn't what?" demanded Claire.

"Nothing. I was just thinking you'd have suited Victorian times."

"You were thinking I'd have suited the role of the daughter, weren't you?" exclaimed Claire. "Well, perhaps you'd like to tell Mike that some time."

Christine flushed, the colour spreading up her neck and over her face. "That wasn't what I meant at all. Becky looks gorgeous in anything."

"Yes, but she couldn't act her way out of a paper bag," said Claire furiously.

"Coffee time!" called Lynne softly. "Mugs are on the table. I couldn't make tea because we've run out of tea bags. Even the milk was off, but Hazel ran down to the 24-hour supermarket and got two cartons."

Claire tugged at the pearl buttons on the bodice of the dress. "I'm dying of thirst. I hope I've got time to have some before Mike calls for the next scene."

When she'd gone Christine looked at Suzanne. "She really minds about the part of the daughter going to Becky, doesn't she?"

Suzanne nodded. "Yes, she does. And so would I in her shoes. She's such a good actress, and with the right make-up and good costumes she could have looked really stunning."

"It's a pity she goes around winding everyone up," said Christine. "If she wasn't so aggressive I'm sure Mike would have considered her for the part, but you must admit she hides her femininity rather well. And the trouble is, Becky is so feminine and beautiful, Mike tends to forget other people's talents."

"I think she's got a severe attitude problem," said Emma. "Someone should point it out to her. Have you finished telling me I'm overweight now? Because I'd like some coffee too and I'm due back on in five minutes." She left the room.

"It's all a bit tense, isn't it," said Suzanne sympathetically.

Christine bit on her bottom lip. "It's horrible. There's no pleasure in it for anyone any more. I'd like Mike to close the play down but he won't hear of it. I keep wondering if anything else is going to happen, and I imagine that's what most of you are thinking."

"Yes," admitted Suzanne. "But really, the worst part is wondering whether the two incidents were connected, and if they were who's behind it. It doesn't seem possible that it's someone we all know."

Hazel put her blonde head round the door. "Suzanne, Emma says to come and get your coffee because Mike wants to go through your scene again next."

"Right, I'll come now!" called Suzanne, and left Christine still trying to expand the waistband on Emma's dress.

"What kept you?" asked Emma, handing Suzanne her coffee mug, which she put on the table.

"We were talking about Claire. I wish they'd had tea bags, I loathe this coffee, it's so bitter."

"I don't care what it tastes like as long as it's wet. I think I've got a cold coming on, my throat's sore and my nose is all stuffy," said Emma, lifting her mug.

The smell of the coffee almost made Suzanne retch, and then, just as Emma put the mug to her lips, Suzanne made a frantic grab at the handle. Emma screamed and the hot liquid slopped over the sides of the mug and down onto the table.

"What on earth are you doing?" she demanded, but Suzanne was watching the liquid collect into a strange oily pool on the table top while the unmistakable smell of turpentine rose and hit the back of her throat.

"Suzie, you could have scalded me!" continued Emma furiously.

"You'd have been more than scalded if I hadn't spilt it," said Suzanne in a shaky voice. "There's turps in that drink, Emma. Can't you smell it?"

"I told you, I've got a stuffy nose," said Emma, but then she lowered her head and sniffed at the muddy liquid carefully. When she lifted her face, her eyes were huge and dark with fright. "You're right," she whispered. "God, Suzie, that could have poisoned me."

The two girls stared at each other in terror across the small table and then instinctively clasped hands. "We'll have to tell Mike," said Suzanne. Emma nodded.

"Suzanne!" called Lynne. "Mike wants you on stage. He's not happy with your opening scene."

Suzanne didn't move from her seat. She was still recovering from the shock of what had nearly happened to Emma and felt sick to her stomach.

"Suzanne!" Lynne rushed up to them. "Mike says hurry up."

"Tell him we need a five-minute break. Emma and I have to speak to him first."

"I don't think that will be very popular," remarked Lynne but she went off to pass on the message.

When the two girls told him what had happened he groaned. "Can't we get any peace round here? What the hell is going on? I'd better take a look at this for myself."

They led him backstage to the small room where the drinks were on the table, but when they got there the table had been wiped clean and the dirty mugs removed. Suzanne and Emma stared at each other. "Who did that?" gasped Emma. "No one ever clears up dirty mugs, not even when it's time to go home."

"Who did what?" asked Hazel, coming in with clean mugs and a fresh supply of coffee.

"Did you clean this table up?" demanded Suzanne.

Hazel looked taken aback by her anger. "Yes, Lynne told me at the last rehearsal to make sure it didn't get too messy in here. Someone had slopped coffee all over the table. It was disgusting. I suppose it was one of the boys."

"Did you notice anything odd about it?" asked Mike quietly.

Hazel's rather vague blue eyes were puzzled. "It seemed rather a thoughtless thing to do," she said. "I mean, no one else could use the table while it was like that."

"What about the spilt coffee?" asked Emma patiently.

Hazel stared blankly at her. "What about it?"

"Nothing," interrupted Mike. "Not to worry, you're doing fine. It makes a change to have someone on their toes all the time. Come on, girls, back to work."

"We didn't make it up, you know," said Suzanne furiously. "Someone put that turps into Emma's coffee on purpose. She's got a cold coming on; they'd have guessed she wouldn't be able to smell it. If I hadn't been there you'd be calling a second ambulance to the hall, and that would probably have been the end of our group."

Mike put a gentle hand on her shoulder. "Ease up there, Suzie. I know it's been difficult for all of you recently, but don't you think that Hazel would have smelt turpentine when she cleared up? I do. No, I honestly believe you overreacted to the smell of cheap coffee! I don't blame you; better safe than sorry, but let's leave it at that, shall we?"

"You're a coward," said Emma quietly. "You believe us really, I know you do, but you're afraid to admit it."

"Rubbish!" Mike laughed nervously.

Suzanne looked at her friend with new respect. If she'd been in Emma's shoes she'd have been in tears by now at Mike's refusal to believe them.

"It doesn't matter," continued Emma. "This

time they failed, next time they probably won't. Unless you close the group down there's nothing you can do, so you might as well go on burying your head in the sand. Actually, I'm not feeling too well with this cold so I think I'll go now. I'll see you all next weekend."

Mike watched her leave. He looked faintly guilty, but not as guilty as Suzanne felt he should. "How could you do that to Emma?" she demanded. "She's one of the most honest people I've ever met."

"I never doubted Emma. It was you who smelt the so-called turpentine. According to your story, Emma would have drunk her coffee if you hadn't knocked it so dramatically from her hand."

"And you think that would have been better? For her to drink turps?" asked Suzanne incredulously.

"Keep your voice down! *There never was any turpentine*. No one smelt it but you, no one would have mentioned it but for you. From what I can gather this group seems to be setting itself up as a bunch of amateur sleuths over all this, and I think it's gone to your head. Stick to the acting, Suzanne. That's something you do quite well."

"Who said we were acting like sleuths?"

Mike sank back into his chair, well aware that most of the group were watching them talking. "I don't think that matters. Just remember that if there really was anything to investigate the police would be doing it. For all you know they're doing something right now, but tactfully; behind the scenes as it were, not crashing around all over the place antagonizing people. Now please, get back on stage."

Suzanne found that she was shaking with fury, and the re-run of her scene went so badly that she felt utterly ashamed. Steven, who was in the scene with her, could see her trembling and wondered what on earth had happened to upset her.

"Right, that's it!" called Mike at six o'clock. "You'd better work on that before Wednesday, Suzie. It's still a little weak." Suzanne ignored him. "As for the rest of you," he continued, "on the whole I'm pleased. We've got ten days before the first of the two dress rehearsals, that's Tuesday week. The next day is the final one, and we perform on the Thursday, Friday and Saturday nights, so start getting the tickets sold."

8

"What on earth's wrong?" asked Steven as Suzanne started to leave the stage.

"I'll talk to you at home," she muttered, too close to tears to be able to stop at that moment.

Before Steven could leave, Mike waylaid him. "Steven, could I have a quick word? I think I upset Suzanne. She and Emma cooked up their own little drama backstage earlier and I rather blew a fuse. You'll appreciate that we've got enough on our plates without the girls letting their imagination run riot. No doubt she'll tell you her side of it, but I honestly think it was a storm in a tea-cup, or perhaps I should say coffee mug!" He gave a short laugh.

Steven looked steadily at him. "Suzanne doesn't

have an overactive imagination, nor does Emma. As for blowing a fuse, you should be keeping everyone calm at the moment. You're meant to be in charge."

"Yes, and while I'm in charge, what I say goes. I'm sure the girls had good reason to *think* there was a problem, but as far as I'm concerned they've blown it out of all proportion, and that's the end of it!" continued Mike before turning away and leaving with Christine.

Steven shrugged his shoulders. At least I tried, he thought ruefully.

Once Steven and Suzanne got home, he wanted to get straight down to talking but she insisted on ringing Emma first. "I'm sorry," said Emma's mother, raising her voice to drown out her small stepdaughter's shouts, "Em's gone to bed. She feels a bit 'fluey, and doesn't want to miss the Maths test tomorrow. Is there any message?"

"No, just tell her I rang and I hope she feels better soon," said Suzanne dejectedly.

Steven was about to drag her off for a talk then, but their mother said tea was ready and it would make a nice change if they ate together as a family for once. So, it was nearly eight o'clock before they were finally alone in Steven's room with a chance to talk privately.

"What happened?" Steven demanded. "I've never seen you look as upset as you did on stage this afternoon."

"That's hardly surprising," said Suzanne, and told him exactly what had gone on behind the scenes.

"But Hazel must have smelt something!" exclaimed Steven when his sister had finished.

"Unless the smell evaporates."

"No, it lingers for hours. Couldn't you still smell it when you took Mike back?"

Suzanne thought for a moment. "No, I couldn't. All I could smell was that foul air freshener, pot-pourri or something, that Christine gets us to spray around before we leave."

"There you are then! Someone deliberately cleared up and then sprayed the room with air freshener."

"But who?"

"Hazel?"

"Why on earth should Hazel be involved in all this?"

Steven shook his head. "I'm not saying she was involved. All I'm saying is that in her zeal to show how efficient she is, she did an extra good job of cleaning that little room up without realizing that she was wiping out all the evidence when she wiped the tabletop."

"She'd still have noticed the smell."

"There are lots of odd smells backstage when we're finishing off the set. Besides, I don't suppose she'd know paint thinner from greasepaint. No, I think you were just very unlucky."

Suzanne slumped down in the chair by Steven's desk. "But even if that's true, Mike behaved abominably. And why is he so annoyed because we're all trying to find out what's going on? He's in charge of the group; doesn't he feel at all guilty about what happened to Richard?"

"You know what he's like. He teaches drama at your school and you always say he's the most dedicated teacher there. It's his first teaching post, the drama group adds to his success and if he wants a department of his own one day he needs to show he's willing to work outside school hours. The group's very important to him."

"The group's important to all of us!" protested Suzanne.

"It isn't the same. I don't think any of us really matter to him individually, only as a group."

"The plays do get good reviews in quite a lot of local papers," admitted Suzanne.

"And if I ever become a famous actor he'll bask in my reflected glory," added Steven.

"I think he's being dead selfish," said Suzanne. "As for Emma, she had the most terrible scare. Isn't there anything the group can do to stop all this before someone else gets killed?"

"I'm starting to have an idea," said Steven slowly, "but I'd rather keep it to myself at the moment because I want you to behave perfectly naturally towards everyone. If I mention my suspicions, I think you'd find that difficult."

"You're not the only one who can act," retorted Suzanne. "What makes you so special?"

"I didn't say I was special. I'll tell you if you like, but I'm probably wrong anyway."

Suzanne put her head in her hands. "It's all so horrible. Just a few weeks ago we were such a happy group. What's happened to change it?"

"That's what I asked myself," said Steven. "If you think about it too and come up with any answers, let me know. I'll be interested to see if our conclusions are the same. In the meantime, be careful."

After Suzanne had left his room, Steven sat with his head in his hands. He'd always suspected that Suzanne resented him a little. Everything had been so much harder for her. Schoolwork, making friends, sport, it had all been an effort.

Since she'd decided to become a nursery nurse and her grades were certainly going to be good enough for that, their parents had stopped pushing her. Steven had assumed she'd been grateful for that, but lately he'd wondered if she'd seen it as a lack of interest on their part. Recently, after the way she behaved when she'd been out with Stuart, and now tonight when she'd snapped at him, he'd begun to wonder about Suzanne's behaviour. He remembered how angry she'd been when Becky had landed the daughter's part in the play. But surely not angry enough to put a dead cat in a box to punish her?

It wasn't only that though. She'd often remarked about Richard's clowning, saying it put her off when she was trying to concentrate. She was his sister and he loved her, but as Claire had pointed out that didn't mean anything.

He was bitterly ashamed of his suspicions, but they lingered. The coffee incident could have been a blind, a way of involving herself without getting hurt. He didn't want it to be true and he hoped that his other line of thought was the right one, but try as he might he couldn't banish the fear entirely.

9

On the night of the first dress rehearsal the group were full of the usual mixture of excited anticipation, panic and laughter as completed costumes were put on for the first time.

"Where's Claire?" asked Christine, holding Claire's dress up in the air. "I've just finished pressing this."

"She isn't here yet," said Stuart from behind the curtain that hung from the ceiling of the small changing room, separating the boys from the girls. "She's at a college union meeting."

"Trust her to be a member of the students' union," remarked Becky. "She's so bossy she'll probably be the next woman Prime Minister."

"It certainly won't be you!" retorted Emma,

struggling to fasten the press-studs round her waist. "It's brains, not beauty, they look for in MPs."

"I find that hard to believe!" laughed Steven.

"Anyway, Mike doesn't select prospective Members of Parliament," whispered Suzanne to Emma, and they both collapsed with giggles.

"That's enough," said Christine, who'd overheard but decided to ignore the remark. "Becky, you look absolutely gorgeous!"

All the other girls turned to look at Becky, standing in her long, white dress trimmed with embroidered pink roses, her hair tumbling loose over her shoulders, and secretly they knew that she did, but not one of them was going to admit it.

"I don't think Victorian women had busts," remarked Lynne seriously, as she collected some props from the far end of the room.

"What do you think they did with them then?" asked Becky sweetly. "Cut them off?"

Lynne blushed. "I just meant that they all look kind of flattened in pictures I've seen."

"You should have got my part then," Becky flashed back, sweeping out of the changing room.

"Catty!" called Steven.

"She was provoked," admitted Suzanne.

"I meant the rest of you," Steven told her. "She can't help looking so lovely."

"No, it must be a frightful curse," said Emma in a bored voice. "Who's going to read in for Claire until she gets here?"

"Mike says Hazel can do it," said Christine, checking all the girls' outfits before sending them on to the stage. "She belongs to your school debating society, doesn't she? She'll be able to read the lines and Claire shouldn't be long."

At that moment Stuart groaned. "Oh, no! The top two buttons on my waistcoat have popped off."

"You'll have to sew them on yourself," said Christine distractedly. "I'm needed backstage to work the sound effects and Lynne's prompting, so with Hazel on stage there isn't anyone else. The needle and thread are on the bench there."

"But I can't sew!" protested Stuart.

"Good time for you to learn," laughed Steven as he hurried out. "Lucky you're not on in the first fifteen minutes. That gives you seven and a half minutes per button."

After the door closed behind Steven, Stuart felt suddenly uneasy now that everyone had gone. He was certain that whoever killed Richard had had a purpose, and probably still had. He could quite easily be a prospective victim himself and the silence in the changing room was unnerving. All at once he longed for Richard to appear, cracking one of his corny jokes and telling him it had all been a trick and he wasn't really dead at all.

His heart beating a little too loudly, Stuart sat down on the narrow bench and reluctantly began to sort out the right coloured thread. When he heard the sound of the door opening he jumped out of his skin and his heart threatened to burst through his chest.

He was about to call out and ask who it was when he heard Claire swear as she tripped over the step into the room. Realizing that he'd been holding his breath he exhaled noisily. "Claire! Thank heavens. Can you sew on buttons?"

For a moment she didn't answer, and all his suspicions of her came flooding back so that he could no longer just sit there and wait for her to appear, he had to get up. At least then he wasn't so vulnerable. He stuck his head out from behind the curtain.

Claire was looking at herself in the full-length mirror that had been put there to check the costumes. She was still wearing the college uniform of jeans and T-shirt and her face was pale. She started as she saw Stuart's face loom up behind her in the mirror and he realized that she was frightened too. For a moment he felt relief, but then he wondered if she was afraid like him or – a terrifying thought – nervous of something she was about to do.

"Are you trying to scare me to death creeping up on me like that?" she snapped furiously.

"Sorry, I thought you'd have heard me call out. Christine's left me to sew on my buttons but I don't know how to do it." He tried to sound casual but his voice was too high and strained.

Claire stared at him. "You're pathetic!" she said shortly. "What will you do when you leave home and Mummy isn't there to sew on your buttons any more?"

Stuart attempted a joke. "Get a girlfriend to do it instead."

"Chauvinist. Girls have better things to do with their time than sew on buttons for feeble boys with no initiative. Haven't you heard of the 'New Man'? He washes up, changes nappies and sews the buttons on for his wife. It's a new world out there. Trouble is, no one's told my stepfather," she added to herself.

"Okay, I only asked. Your dress is hanging up at the end. Christine seems to have put a lot of work into it."

"Trying to make me look lovely, I expect. Waste of time now, isn't it? Mike will never see past Becky when the script says 'a beautiful young girl'. I wouldn't mind but she can't act," she finished through clenched teeth.

For the first time, Stuart felt sorry for Claire. He hadn't realized quite how much she minded losing the part of the daughter. "But you're terrific as her mother," he said sincerely. "Everyone will be able to see that you're the one who can really act."

For a moment Claire's face lost its mask of disdain and she looked very vulnerable. "I know, but just for once I'd like to have looked beautiful. Pathetic and against everything I believe in, but there it is. Are you going to stand there gawping while I change? I thought you had buttons to sew on."

Stuart hastily dived back to his side of the curtain. His fear of Claire was almost gone. Just then he heard a sound at the door. "That must be Christine. Don't say I'm due on already." He glanced at his watch. "No, I've still got five minutes; I wonder who it was. Aagh! I've pricked myself with the needle now."

Claire pulled a face as she stepped out of her jeans and T-shirt and reached for the dress. "Baby!" Then she stopped, lifting her head slightly.

"Stuart, can you smell something strange?"

"Probably my socks!"

"I'm serious, idiot."

Stuart sniffed the air. "Yes, kippers or something smokey like that."

Claire opened her mouth to tell him that no one was likely to be eating kippers on stage and immediately began to cough. "It isn't kippers," she said in astonishment. "It's smoke. Where's it coming from?"

Stuart pushed the curtain aside, and for once Claire didn't scream at him although she was in the middle of changing. "It's from the far end, I think. The lights have gone down there, so you can't really see. Perhaps there's a bonfire outside."

"But there's no window in here. How could the smell get in? Stuart, it's getting worse," she added, her voice rising in alarm.

Slowly, out of the gloom from the far end of the room, tiny spirals of smoke began to emerge, creeping into the lighted area and making them both cough. Stuart ran into the darkened section but had to beat a quick retreat as dense smoke entered his nostrils, hurting his throat.

"I think it's coming from the costume box. I daren't open it or it will really go up in flames. Is there an extinguisher in here?" he asked urgently.

Claire immediately reached up onto the shelf above the mirror. "Yes, I saw one here last weekend. Blast! it's gone!"

"We'd better get out and tell the others. There's a large extinguisher in the wings. Come on, it's getting a bit nasty here." By now the smoke was beginning to fill the small room and both of them were spluttering, with tears streaming from their eyes.

"Open the door!" hissed Claire, standing just behind him, but Stuart's hand failed to turn the doorknob and his stomach lurched as he suddenly realized that the noise he'd heard earlier must have been someone locking the door from the outside.

"I can't!" he said in horror.

"Don't be so feeble!" Claire pushed him out of the way and struggled furiously with the handle. "It seems to have jammed." She started to hammer on the door.

"I don't think it's jammed," said Stuart frantically. "I thought I heard someone at the door just after you arrived. I'm afraid they were actually locking it."

"You mean we've been shut in here with this smoke deliberately? But how could anyone have started a fire without us knowing?"

"Don't ask me! I didn't do it!" Stuart was getting as angry as Claire now, and they were both coughing, their breath rasping and burning in their throats as the smoke continued to engulf the room.

"Should we lie on the floor?" asked Claire. "Doesn't smoke rise or something? I remember reading that you get the most air by lying on the floor."

"We'll get the most air by getting the hell out of here. Come on, just hammer and scream as loud as you can."

"They won't hear," said Claire flatly. "There'll be too much noise on stage." She stared at Stuart despairingly.

"They've got to hear," said Stuart firmly. Together they began to beat on the door, at the same time shouting as loudly as their smoke-filled lungs would let them.

On stage, Steven was anxious about Claire. He'd known she was going to be late, but not this late and anyway he'd been certain he'd seen her going up the steps to the wings about ten minutes earlier. Hazel was reading the lines well enough, but it was Claire he liked to act with, Claire who brought the scene to life. His attention began to wander.

"Prompt!" shouted Mike. Hazel quickly fed Steven his line.

Steven picked it up for a few words, and then lost it again.

"What's the matter with you?" demanded Mike. "You knew it all last Sunday."

Steven turned his head towards the dressing room. "I can hear something backstage. Shut up everyone."

"The first thing a real actor needs is the ability to give 100 per cent concentration all the time," said Mike pompously.

Steven ignored him. Now that the music had stopped he could quite clearly hear muffled thumps and the sound of feeble shouts. He could also smell smoke. "Something's wrong back there!" he yelled, and dashed from the stage closely followed by Chris, Emma and Becky.

Christine dropped the prompt book and ran round the back of the stage while Hazel remained where she was, the script still clutched in her hand.

As the group reached the dressing room door they could see the smoke pouring from beneath it, and now Stuart and Claire's cries were clearly audible. Steven tried to turn the handle. "It's locked! Where's the key?" he demanded.

"That door's never locked," said Christine.

"It is now. For heaven's sake, where's the key?"

There was general panic, with the girls crying out and the boys pushing and shoving in a useless attempt to force the door. "Here it is!" called Christine suddenly. "It was lying on the floor right under my feet."

Steven grabbed it from her, turned it in the lock and shouted, "It's open now!" as loudly as he could.

Inside the smoke-filled room Claire and Stuart glanced at each other in heart-stopping relief. Then Stuart pulled open the door and they both fell out, coughing and spluttering, into their friends' arms.

Mike dashed straight through with the large fire extinguisher, quickly locating the costume box as the source of the problem and covering it in an all-enveloping layer of foam.

As he worked, the rest of the group led the terrified Stuart and Claire into the main body of the hall, opening the doors and windows as they went to let in the fresh air.

Claire slumped in a chair and Steven sat beside

her, putting an arm round her shoulders and wiping a smoke-mark from her tear-stained face. "It's all right," he said softly. "You're safe now."

"I thought we were going to die!" she blurted out, and then she finally began to cry as Steven pulled her head down to rest on his shoulder.

"You're all right," he repeated calmly, but inside he didn't feel at all calm. He had no doubt in his mind that both Claire and Stuart had been meant to die.

The dress rehearsal was abandoned. They all helped to tidy up as best they could and the costume box was brought out for them to examine.

"Full of burnt paper beneath the clothes," said Mike. "Slow to take hold but potentially lethal if either of you had opened the box. Thank heavens you had more sense."

For a brief moment, Steven and Suzanne were alone together. "I think the culprit's beginning to lose control," whispered Steven, "and we can't stop them because we don't know what their motive is."

"Whoever it is they must be totally mad," replied Suzanne furiously. "Mike *has* to call the police."

At last Mike turned to face the group. "I don't think there's any choice any more," he said slowly. "This was attempted murder. I shall have to call in the police."

Suzanne glanced at her brother in satisfaction.

10

Suzanne and Steven had told their parents about the near-tragedy at the dress rehearsal as soon as they got home. Their mother kept saying that now the group had to close, while their father, once he'd reassured himself that both his children were unhurt, had another fear.

"You can't afford to get involved with the police if you're going to be a solicitor," he said to Steven with a worried frown.

"Dad, I'm a witness to a crime, that's all. Anyway, I'm not going to be a solicitor. I'm going to be an actor."

"I'd have thought these past few weeks would have put you off that for good. Look what happens when you mix with stage people."

Suzanne laughed despite what had happened to them. "These are our school friends, or teenagers from the college, not 'stage people'. And you can get sick people in any walk of life."

Their mother looked very put out. "Sick? Who said anyone was sick? It seems to me you've got a troublemaker in the group but Mike's let it get out of hand, that's all."

Steven shook his head, watching their mother go back into the kitchen still muttering to herself. "She'll do anything rather than face the truth about things. Do you know, the other day she said she wished I was more like you!" he told Suzanne.

"And wanted to become a nursery nurse?" giggled Suzanne.

"That's what I said, but of course I got told off for answering back. Trouble is, it's true that everything that's been happening to the group hasn't exactly helped my cause as a would-be actor."

When the police arrived it was the same Detective Sergeant who had talked to them when Richard died. This time he'd brought along a different WPC, and he seemed more alert, as though he now believed there was a job for the police to do.

"I'd like to see Steven and Suzanne on their own, Mrs Parkin, if you don't mind," he said. "Perhaps the young lady first?"

"I think I should be there too," said Mrs Parkin anxiously.

"Oh no, Mum!" exclaimed Suzanne. "I'd rather you weren't."

"The WPC will be there," said Detective Sergeant Martin and so, reluctantly, Mrs Parkin left the three of them alone in the front room.

"Right," said the policeman with a brief reassuring smile at Suzanne. "How about you telling me everything that's been happening to your little group since young Richard died."

Suzanne, who resented them being referred to as a little group, told him it all in as factual a way as possible, only getting agitated when she described the incident with Emma's drink. "I know it wasn't the worst thing to happen," she apologized, "but it was the shock of being there and realizing that she could have been badly hurt, or even died."

"Of course, anyone would find it distressing. I'd like you to be perfectly honest with me, Suzanne. Have you any idea who could be behind all this?"

Suzanne shook her head. "No, none at all. I mean, we've all been affected at some stage, which makes it very difficult."

"Not quite all," the Detective Sergeant interrupted.

"What do you mean?"

His voice was soft. "I mean that both you and

your brother have emerged unscathed from all these so-called accidents."

Suzanne stared at him in silence. He watched her, waiting for a reply, but she couldn't think what to say.

"You seem shocked," he said at last. "Surely you must have thought of it yourself?"

"No, no I hadn't," she protested, although she had. "You see, when things are happening all round you, to your friends and people you've known for some time, it *seems* personal. Stuart's my brother's best friend, and Emma's mine; when they got involved it was like being involved ourselves."

"But nothing *has* happened to either of you, has it?" he pressed her.

Suzanne felt close to tears. "There's nothing I can do about that! I can't ask whoever's behind it all to try and kill one of us, and I don't want to either."

The policeman's shrewd grey eyes continued to watch her closely. "Of course not. But does it suggest anything to you? Can you come up with any reason why you two should have escaped and no one else?"

"We aren't the only ones!" Suzanne said hotly. "Nothing's happened to Lynne or James either."

"Or to Mike and Christine," admitted the policeman.

"That's right! But then, they're not the same as

us. I mean, if someone's got a grudge against the group it's probably directed against his or her colleagues, not Mike and Christine, who run it."

"I'd have thought they'd have been a prime target. It's their drama group. The ultimate responsibility for everything is theirs, isn't it?"

"I don't know what you mean, 'ultimate responsibility'."

"I mean that they have the final say about casting, costumes, who acts as prompt, *who makes the coffee*. Quite important decisions in the light of what's happened."

"I suppose so. I hadn't thought of it like that." Suzanne was thoroughly confused. She was being made to feel guilty because no one had yet tried to kill her. "I didn't do any of this!" she said suddenly. "I don't know what you're thinking but neither Steven nor I have anything to do with it. We both love the group; the last thing we'd want is for it to close."

"Of course," he said smoothly. "I wasn't for one moment suggesting anything else. I only wondered if you could come up with any reason for your good fortune. I shall be asking Lynne Walters and James Desmond the same question. Right, if you've nothing else that you think we should know about, then I'll have a word with that brother of yours. Thank you for your co-operation, miss."

* * *

As soon as Steven sat down opposite the Detective Sergeant he sensed some kind of antagonism in the air. He waited, knowing it was best to let the policeman speak first.

"I understand you're a clever young man," said the Detective Sergeant.

"I don't know about that. I'm in the middle of studying for my A Levels, but I'm not planning to go on to university or anything. I want to be a professional actor."

"Really?" The policeman looked mildly amused. "Like Sir Anthony Hopkins, I suppose?"

"If I could ever be half as good I'd be pleased."

"Interesting. I'm not keen on theatre or films myself, I prefer a good book, but as I recollect he's pretty famous for playing a psychopath, while I hear on the grapevine you've been busy playing detective, isn't that right?"

Steven managed a small smile. "Hardly playing detective. Naturally all the group have talked about what's been going on among themselves, but we haven't attempted to solve the mysteries. That would have been stupid, and possibly dangerous."

"It certainly looks that way now," agreed the policeman. "Have you been convinced all along that malice was behind everything? The dead cat, the accident to Richard? Did you think events were more complicated than they seemed?"

"No, but slowly we all began to wonder. Things

just didn't feel right. I can't explain."

"These things are always best left to the police, you know."

"But you weren't involved! The coroner said Richard's death was an accident, and you were never interested in the dead cat. Leaving it to you meant leaving it alone. We weren't willing to do that, so we talked to each other. That's not a crime."

The policeman was not pleased. Steven knew as soon as he'd spoken that he should have kept quiet. "We're interested now," remarked the Detective Sergeant sharply. "We're interested in everything. All the little rivalries in the group. All the quarrels, backstage gossip, and above all we're interested in why you and your sister haven't been involved in any of these apparent accidents."

Unlike Suzanne, Steven wasn't thrown by the remark. "I've thought about that too," he said. "Either we're not involved in whatever motive or imaginary grudge the person behind all this has, or our turn is still to come."

"Very clever!" said Detective Sergeant Martin, looking far from pleased. "Naturally you've talked to your sister about this?"

"No, I haven't. I nearly did, but then I thought she'd only worry all the time, waiting for something to happen to her. It seemed kinder to keep quiet. I don't think she's ever considered it herself."

"No, it seems not. Since you've all played the detective, if only verbally, perhaps you'd be kind enough to share the fruits of your labours with me. Do you personally have any idea who's behind all this, Steven? If you do then it's your duty to tell us now. Keeping anything back from the police is a criminal offence, as a clever lad like you would know already from the television!" He smiled, but without humour.

"I honestly haven't a clue," said Steven. "If I had I'd have tried to put a stop to all this before Stuart and Claire got caught in the changing room."

The policeman nodded. "Right, well that's all for now then. I think from here on you'd better leave the detective work to us. We'll be working on it now, chatting to everyone, getting the feel of the group as it were. You can concentrate on your A Levels and the acting. It will be quite a relief, I imagine."

Steven knew that the policeman didn't like him and was deliberately trying to irritate him, but he smiled politely back. "It certainly will. So, we're all safe in your hands from now on, are we?"

"Just having us around might put an end to everything," said the policeman, relaxing slightly as the interview was over. "Quite often the very fact that the police have been called in scares off this kind of malicious hoaxer. I can promise you we'll be pretty visible too – lots of interviews, someone in the hall during the final dress rehearsal, all high-profile work."

"But will you ever catch the person responsible?" asked Steven.

"I think you can leave that to us."

"Richard died," said Steven as he got up to go. "I want the person who killed him caught because if they're not, one day they might do the same thing again."

"Our feelings exactly. Thank you for your help, and remember, from now on leave it all to us, agreed?"

"Of course," said Steven.

Later, Steven and Suzanne watched the Detective Sergeant and the silent WPC drive away from the house. "He's suspicious of us!" said Suzanne indignantly. "I'm sure he thinks we're behind it all."

"No, he doesn't. He hasn't a clue what it's about; that's why he's cross," said Steven scornfully. "All he could say was that 'high-profile' policing would put an end to everything. When I pressed him about trying to catch the person responsible he went very vague indeed."

"But you've got an idea who's responsible, haven't you?" asked Suzanne.

"I thought I had, and I was going to tell you," admitted Steven slowly. "The trouble is, now I'm not so sure. The one thing I am sure of is this:

whatever Detective Sergeant Martin has to say, I still believe it's something we have to solve ourselves before someone else is murdered.

"Tonight we'll try and have a meeting of the whole group round at James's house. His parents are always out, and I want to hear what that policeman had to say to everyone, and what they told him."

11

All the members of the Future Drama Group were at James Desmond's house by half-past seven that evening. Suzanne arrived with Emma, and Steven with Stuart.

"I wish they'd call the whole thing off and close the group down," Emma confessed to Suzanne as they arrived. "I've had enough, and I should think Stuart and Claire have too."

"Then that's what you must say," Suzanne told her. "Everyone tonight must give their opinion, and then we can make a decision after that."

"We can't really, not without Mike and Christine here," Emma pointed out.

"I think we can. After all, we're the ones being injured – not them."

Steven took over the running of the meeting and began by asking if anyone had anything they wanted to discuss with the group about their visit from the police.

Claire lifted her hand. "I'd like to say something." Steven nodded encouragingly. "The Detective Sergeant was a bit odd over you and Suzanne," Claire said awkwardly. "He kept asking me if I could think of any reason why neither of you had been hurt."

"He asked me that too!" exclaimed Stuart.

There was a general murmur of agreement from everyone there except Lynne. "He didn't say anything like that to me," she said quietly.

"I don't see how he could," said Emma. "After all, so far you've escaped as well, haven't you?"

Lynne looked as though she might burst into tears. "How dare you say that!" she shouted. "I know I've not been hurt, but that doesn't mean I'm involved. You can't possibly think I am. Anyway, James hasn't been hurt either."

Emma sighed. "I didn't say it was you. I was only pointing out that the police couldn't really comment about Steven and Suzie being unharmed to you, when you've escaped as well."

"I'm just grateful I *have* escaped," confessed James. "I hadn't thought that it might make the police suspect me. They certainly didn't give me that impression, but they did ask why I thought

Suzanne and Steven had both been left alone."

There was an awkward pause. Eventually Stuart spoke. "I think it might be because there are two of them. They're often together. The rest of us are probably easier to get at. Personally, I no longer think any of this has been directed at the individuals concerned. I think it's directed at the group. If that's true then obviously the person will attack whoever is to hand, and that will rarely be Steven and Suzanne. If you think about it, Steven is there less often than the rest of us because of his studying."

"Well, I'm there just as often as Emma or Claire," said Suzanne.

"Perhaps the mug of coffee was meant for you," said Emma suddenly. "It's dark backstage. I could have picked up the wrong mug. Maybe it was pure luck whether it was you or me that time."

"That's a good point," said Steven. "I'd thought of it myself. Were the two mugs side by side, Emma?"

She thought for a moment. "Not exactly; one of them was more towards me but that's only because I sat on the far side of the table. If I'd sat where Suzie did then I'd have picked up the other mug."

"Seems pretty obvious it was a random attack then," agreed James. "It's the same with Richard, really. Claire says he tripped and that's why he took the full force of the flat when it fell, but it could have been anyone on stage that day, and that includes Steven. In all the panic anyone could have tripped or become rooted to the spot."

"What you're saying is that although it hasn't been Steven or Suzanne so far, it could have been?" asked Claire. "Am I right?"

"It looks like that," Lynne said.

"Well, it doesn't apply to you," said Claire sharply. "You weren't backstage drinking coffee, you were busy brewing it up, and you weren't on stage because you can't act."

"Meaning what?" asked Lynne, her face draining of all colour.

"Meaning what's your excuse?"

Steven cleared his throat. "I don't think Lynne needs an excuse not to have been hurt, Claire. Nor does James."

"I'm beginning to wish I *had* been hurt!" exclaimed Lynne to Hazel, who looked sympathetic.

"You're welcome to my place in the changing room," Claire retorted.

"Or mine!" added Stuart. "I never want to go through anything like that again."

"Look, this really isn't the point of the meeting," said Steven crossly. "Do any of you think the police are near to catching whoever's behind all this? Did Detective Sergeant Martin say anything that made you feel confident we were going to be safer from now on?"

"He said the police would be keeping a close watch on everything," Hazel replied. "I thought that was nice."

"Nice!" Claire's eyes were wide with astonishment. "You think it's *nice* of them to try and stop us being choked to death or flattened by scenery? I think they're disgraceful. At first they wouldn't take it seriously, and now they just go round trying to stir things up by asking why some of us haven't been hurt. If you ask me, they're hoping we'll do their work for them."

"I've got a feeling they'll just close us down," said James.

"And let the guilty party get away with everything?" asked Emma indignantly.

"They seem to think that what's done is done, and although they might catch the person next time they can't take that risk. Mike and Christine are at the police station this evening, talking it over, but the last I heard the play was probably going to be abandoned."

"That's not fair!" exclaimed Becky. "My family have all bought tickets."

"In that case I'm sure the police will agree to let the performance go ahead," said Claire acidly. "They'd hardly dare deprive the local population of the opportunity of seeing you display your vast range of acting skills."

"It isn't just me," said Becky sulkily. "I know

you're jealous, but I didn't give myself the part. It was Mike's decision."

Close as he was becoming to her, Steven felt like shaking Claire. He wanted the group as united as possible tonight, not bickering about old scores. "Pack it in, Claire," he said mildly. "Most of us feel the same as Becky."

Claire flushed while Becky flashed Steven one of her most beguiling smiles.

"I don't think there's much more to be gained by talking about it all," Stuart put in. "I think what we should do is take a vote on whether or not we want to continue and then give the result to Mike and Christine. As for putting our faith in the police, well, I'm sure they'll do their best but I for one am going to remain very much on my guard."

"Fine, we'll vote then, but rather than a show of hands we'd better do it on paper. That way no one will feel inhibited by going against the general feeling of the group."

He handed out sheets of paper from his notebook and James got them all pencils. "Put a tick if you want to go on with the play and a cross if you don't," said Steven. "I'll count them up and then one of the girls can double check. Emma, would you do that?"

"Do we have to put our names on the paper?" asked Lynne.

Claire groaned. "That would rather defeat the object of the exercise, stupid!"

"No," said Steven quickly. "Just a tick or a cross."

They all crouched over their pieces of paper, made their mark then folded them up and put them in a jar that James provided, leaving Steven to empty it and count while the others chatted among themselves.

"Okay," he said at last, his voice strained. "I'll tell you what I've got. Five ticks, three crosses and one spoilt paper."

Suzanne frowned at her brother. "What do you mean, one spoilt paper?"

Slowly and with obvious reluctance, Steven held up a sheet from his notebook. On it was a small, neatly drawn skull, the teeth seeming to grin mockingly at them all.

One of the girls screamed. Emma gave a gasp of horror while Suzanne felt sick and James and Stuart turned to each other in consternation. Lynne began to weep silently, and Hazel put a comforting arm round her shoulders.

"If this was a joke it was a pretty sick one," said Steven, "but just about acceptable as long as the artist owns up now. Come on, which of you did this?"

In the long silence that followed his question, all that could be heard was the ticking of the clock on James's bedroom wall.

The whole atmosphere in the room changed. They were no longer a drama group, meeting up to discuss all that had happened in a relatively detached way. Instead they were eight frightened individuals, shaken to the core by the reminder that one of them, someone who had sat there all the evening behaving as normally as the rest, was behind everything that had happened.

For most of them it was the first time they'd fully accepted the terrible truth. During the meeting they'd been relatively relaxed, chatting to their closest friends and exchanging ideas freely.

Now they knew that someone's closest friend was a killer. This wasn't a joke, a malicious prank; this was a message from Richard's killer, and the killer was sitting there pretending to be shocked just like everyone else.

It was impossible now to ignore the real horror that was in their midst. One of them in that room was a murderer.

12

Mike rang Steven the next morning. "Christine and I spent a couple of hours with the police last night. They don't seem convinced there's any real malice behind these incidents, and an Inspector Thompson told me that as far as they're concerned Richard's death was definitely an accident."

"Which means what exactly?" asked Steven.

"Which means that if you all want the play to go on, it can."

"Well, we do. We had a meeting last night and took a vote on it."

"How did the voting go?" asked Mike.

"Five wanted to go on, three didn't and one of us drew a skull. We don't know who; it was a secret ballot."

"Great, then it goes on!" exclaimed Mike.

"Did you hear what I said?" asked Steven. "*Someone drew a skull*."

"People do silly things when feelings run high. I don't suppose it meant anything."

"But of course it did!" Steven lowered his voice so that his parents couldn't hear. "One of us at that meeting wanted to make it clear that not only were they behind everything but also they hadn't finished yet. It was horrible."

"Better stop holding meetings then," said Mike after a pause. "Look, in another few days it will all be over. We can't quit now. Everything's organized. A WPC is sitting in on the dress rehearsal tomorrow. The local council have been very good and agreed we can give our final performance on the Sunday since we won't open until Friday."

"Great!" said Steven, and put down the phone.

"Honestly," he complained to Suzanne later, "he doesn't care about the safety of the group at all, just about putting on the play. By Sunday there probably won't be enough of us alive to do a final performance."

"Stop it," said Suzanne sharply. "You're being silly now. With the police around and everyone on their guard I don't think anything more will happen."

"After that skull," said Steven, "I'm more certain than ever that something will."

*　　*　　*

The final dress rehearsal was not a great success. All of the group were very aware of the WPC sitting next to Mike. Although she was wearing jeans and a sweatshirt, she remained conspicuous because normally no outsiders were allowed in at this stage.

"Think of her as a practice audience," urged Christine when Emma and Suzanne complained. "If she enjoys it, that's a good sign."

"And if she doesn't?" asked Emma.

Christine smiled. "She's got no taste! Come on, you two, I always rely on you to keep things on an even keel. Becky's having an attack of stage fright, which isn't helped by Claire's snide comments about her acting. Emma, would you ask Lynne to make extra sure she's quick coming in with the prompt when Becky hesitates, but that she allows for Claire's dramatic pauses."

"I'd hate to prompt," said Suzanne. "You can never please people and it's murder concentrating for such long periods of time."

"Don't use that word," said Christine with a shiver.

Suzanne looked at Christine closely. Beneath her make-up her face looked strained. "You're really frightened, aren't you?" Suzanne asked softly.

Christine nodded. "Yes, I am. I didn't want the play to go on, but it means so much to Mike."

"You wrote it, it should mean more to you."

"I know, but I've just heard that I've got a job with a publishing firm that specializes in new plays. That means I'll have a good chance of getting them to look at mine in the future. It's different for Mike; he needs this kind of experience to move up the teaching ladder. He's very ambitious."

So Steven had been right, thought Suzanne to herself. Mike needed the group to do well, for his own purposes.

"I'm glad about your new job," she said. "You deserve success and this play's good. I think Mike's dead selfish though."

"Your brother and Claire really make the most of the play," said Christine. "I couldn't have asked for two better actors in their parts. I know Claire wanted to play the daughter, but Becky could never have played the mother and that role has to be done well if the play's to work."

"Have you told Claire that?" Suzanne asked.

"Several times, but I don't think she believes me. Why isn't she going to try for a career on the stage? She's almost as good as Steven."

"I'm not sure," said Suzanne. "I think she has to start earning money. Her stepfather's out of work, he has been for ages, and she hates her mother having to work the night-shift at the food factory."

Just then, Hazel hurried in. "Suzanne, you're wanted, and you, Becky. Mike's going to do a lighting check before he begins and asked for you both."

Claire watched Becky leave, her long white dress clinging to her curves and her hair glinting even in the dim backstage light. "I could kill for looks like that," she said quietly.

Steven was standing at her elbow. "I don't think you mean that, Claire," he said gently. "Becky is beautiful, but that's all she's got. Think how awful it will be when she grows older and there's nothing left."

"I'd chance it."

"Claire, you are coming to the last-night party with me, aren't you?" asked Steven, unusually hesitant for him. Claire nodded, her thoughts still miles away. "Great! I could call for you about eight at your house, if you like."

Claire's eyes lit up and a blush of colour added softness to her features. Then the light seemed to dim. "Of course I'm coming with you," she said, "but don't bother calling for me. It's always hectic at home on Sundays. I'll meet you outside the Blue Pig; it's just up the road from us, unfortunately."

"Whatever suits you best," Steven assured her, delighted that she was letting him continue to get closer to her, and break through the surface cynicism that so often made her difficult and un-approachable. He'd never felt this way about a girl before.

"Making a date?" asked Stuart with a grin once Claire had left.

"Yes, if you must know. How about you? Are you taking anyone special?"

"I hoped Suzanne might come with me, but you know what she's like. She doesn't want to upset Emma so they'll probably go together and the pair of them will stick to each other like glue the whole evening. I won't get a chance to be alone with her at all. I don't know why girls bother to go to parties if they're only going to talk to the same friend they see every day of their lives when they're at school," he added disconsolately.

"I think Suzanne would rather go with you; it's just she's been friends with Emma such a long time, and I think it's difficult for her," Steven told him. "Just don't ask now. She gets very nervous at dress rehearsals."

"I've been very nervous ever since I got locked in the changing room," Stuart commented. Before they could talk any more they were called on stage, and the final dress rehearsal got underway in earnest.

"Not too bad," said Mike grudgingly, two hours later. "We need to knock about half an hour off the running time, but that mess-up in Scene Two when Becky skipped to Scene Three by mistake and you all had to go back added quite a bit on, and the scene changes took far too long. I hope you'll have that ironed out by tomorrow night. Christine?"

She shouted something that might have been an assurance from the wings.

"I'm sorry about the mix-up over scenes," said Becky, sitting down gracefully on the nearest arm-chair. "The trouble is so many of the words are alike."

"I know," Claire agreed. "There are lots of 'and's' and 'but's' which must confuse you. The fact that one minute you were talking about want-ing to meet a young man, and then straight away started gushing on about his charms before he'd even put in an appearance didn't seem to trouble you though!"

Everyone laughed. Becky flushed scarlet. "It was a mistake. You're not perfect; you had to have two prompts."

Claire darted a look of malice at the hapless Lynne sitting in the wings. "Actually, I didn't need any. Lynne simply forgot to allow for the pauses."

"I'm sorry!" Lynne shouted out. "It's a horrible job, I never wanted it in the first place, but no one else volunteered. Some of you want quick prompts, some of you like time to think . . ."

"And some of us are just pausing for effect!" said Claire icily.

"Normally I'd ask for another run-through," said

Mike, "but unfortunately there isn't time tonight."

The group were amazed, then Steven noticed the plain-clothes WPC looking at her watch and realized that she must have to go and that Mike wasn't willing to take the risk of having anything happen when she wasn't there.

"All I can say now is: good luck tomorrow. I know it will be a great success and I'm very proud of you all."

At that the main lights came up, the stage lights were dimmed and the cast started to troop off.

"You forgot to give me my cue at the beginning of the second act," Stuart complained to Emma.

"I know! My mind went a complete blank; it was awful. The trouble was I thought I heard a sort of creaking noise and I kept wondering if something was going to fall on top of us."

"I heard that too," said Chris. "I was right in the middle of my opening speech when I first noticed it and I couldn't help but remember that must have been the point in the play when Richard was killed."

Steven frowned. "How long did the noise go on?"

"For ages," said Emma. "If it started when Chris was talking and I heard it in the second act, that's a pretty long time."

"I didn't hear it and I was on stage most of the time," said Becky.

"Yes, but front left. Chris and I spend most of our time front right."

Steven stopped in his tracks. "I think we'd better go and check the scenery down there, just to make sure."

Steven, Stuart, Emma and Chris left the rest of the group and went back onto the stage. All around them people were closing windows and getting the hall as straight as possible.

The three lads tested the door-frame, and also the join in that section of the backdrop. Everything seemed secure. It was only when they were coming away that Chris noticed the small tape recorder lying on the floor, hidden by the stage curtain.

"What's that used for?" he asked, picking it up.

Emma shook her head. "I've no idea. All the sound effects come from the other side. Christine does them."

Steven took the tape recorder from Chris and rewound the cassette. Then he pushed the "Play" button and waited. After a moment they were astounded to hear a series of soft creaking noises, like a door hinge that needed oiling. From time to time there would be a silence, and then more creaks which continued until the cassette ran out.

"Someone put that there on purpose, just to frighten us!" said Emma furiously.

"It's a rotten thing to do, but otherwise it's harmless," Stuart pointed out.

"If you ask me, it's really sick," said Steven, tight-lipped with anger. "Sounds like that were bound to distract anyone within earshot, and bring back memories of poor Richard. And what a slap in the eye for the police. They have a WPC sitting out front, and our murderer puts a tape recorder down, then leaves it running right under her nose."

"But why?" asked Emma. "Apart from making us nervous and possibly fluffing our lines, what possible point is there in doing something like that?"

"I'd have thought that was obvious," said Steven. "It's made certain that we all know nothing has changed. Not even the police are going to stop this nightmare until someone manages to catch the perpetrator in the act."

"The act of what?" asked Emma.

No one dared to imagine what the answer might be.

13

There was always tension and excitement on an opening night, Suzanne reflected, but this time there was an added ingredient: fear. All of them, with the exception of the person responsible for the entire nightmare, were very frightened.

It was Claire who had voiced what was uppermost in their minds when she walked into the hall and surveyed the rows of empty chairs waiting for the ticket-holders. "With an audience like that, how is our friend going to be able to resist putting on a really special performance for them?" she asked Emma.

Emma shivered. "Don't talk about it tonight, please, Claire. It's as much as I can do to concentrate as it is."

"As long as we stay on our guard we should be all right. Is the WPC here?" she added.

"I haven't seen her," said Emma. "Perhaps she's blending in."

"With what? The scenery? Come off it. There aren't many places she could go and blend, except in the audience, of course. I suppose that's where she'll hide. A fat lot of use that will be."

Hazel hurried up to them, looking anxious and flustered. "Come on you two. Christine wants all the cast to report backstage for make-up as soon as they arrive, otherwise she won't get finished in time."

"You like being bossy, don't you!" said Claire in a detached way.

Hazel chewed on her bottom lip. "No I don't, but there's so much to do, and Lynne isn't concentrating properly because she's so scared, which means it's all being left to me."

"It's only a local drama group, not the Royal Shakespeare Company," Emma soothed her but Hazel, tense-faced and pale, rushed off to carry out some other task.

"She's a bit weird tonight," remarked Claire. "James! You haven't finished painting the window frame yet, you idiot."

James ambled over to them, paint brush in hand. "I did it yesterday, but someone brushed up against it while it was wet. I'm just about to give it a last going over, only for heaven's sake stay away from it."

Claire ignored the last comment and went off to Christine for make-up, leaving Emma and James alone.

He smiled at her. "Have you thought any more about coming to the party with me, Em? Now that Steven and Claire are an item I . . ." He saw the look of surprise in her eyes and stopped. He'd been sure she must have found out by now.

After a long silence, Emma nodded. "If you still want to take me, I don't mind. My stepfather will take us in the car if we want a lift. He and Mum are coming on the last night so they can easily drop us off."

"Sounds cool. I'll walk you home, then they needn't worry about you getting back safely."

Emma, her worst fears about Steven and Claire confirmed, tried to make the best of it. She decided that James was better looking than she'd at first thought, and perhaps there was a slight resemblance to Mel Gibson after all. He was a good group member as well, always helping backstage and giving a reliable performance in character parts. She knew Suzanne would go with Stuart in the end and she certainly didn't want to turn up alone. She tried not to think about what it would have been like to go with Steven.

During the next hour the tension mounted. They

all got into their costumes, and heard the steadily rising hum of the voices from the audience as the chairs filled up.

As usual, Mike came round to wish them luck before going to his seat in the back row. He always said that he liked to make sure everyone who'd paid for a ticket could hear every word, and that was the best way of finding out.

After he'd gone, none of the actors were supposed to leave the dressing room again before going on stage. Chris, who was required to take out a fob-watch from his pocket in the first scene, suddenly discovered that he'd left it on the table round the other side of the stage.

"I'll have to get it, Christine," he pointed out. "There's no one here who isn't an actor. Besides, Lynne and Hazel are rushed off their feet, you know they are."

"You're not going on your own," said Christine firmly, busy applying make-up to Emma's face. "Becky, you're finished so you can go with Chris. That way I can be quite sure of getting the pair of you back in one piece."

"Where's the representative from the local force?" muttered Emma from under the greasepaint.

"Keep still!" ordered Christine. "I've no idea where she is. Out front, I expect."

Chris and Becky promised they'd only be five minutes and crept cautiously round the back of the set. There were always things to fall over and odd brushes and paint tins lying around that could mess up their costumes so they were extra careful. To their surprise, they found Hazel sitting at the table. She was looking straight at them, but she didn't speak and it was difficult to see the expression in her eyes because it was so dark.

"I left my fob-watch there," said Chris softly, afraid of his voice carrying out into the hall. "Could you pass it to me?"

"We thought you backstage lot were rushed off your feet!" added Becky with a laugh. "Don't let Lynne catch you sitting down drinking coffee with only five minutes before curtain up!"

Hazel didn't answer them. She simply continued to sit there. Chris reached out towards the table trying to find the watch and accidentally moved it a little to one side. Immediately Hazel toppled from her chair, crashing to the ground in an awkward tangle of limbs and table legs.

Becky screamed and Chris groped his way forward. "She must have fainted. Quick, get a torch or something, and fetch Christine. She's responsible for first aid."

"Suppose she's dead!" wailed Becky.

"Don't be stupid! Why should she be dead?"

"What's going on?" demanded Lynne, hurrying round from the prompt corner. "Becky, your scream could be heard everywhere. Where's Hazel?

I asked her to get me a drink ages ago and she hasn't brought it yet."

"She seems to have fainted," said Chris, bending down, but as his hands touched Hazel's body they also encountered something hard sticking out from between her shoulder-blades and his fingers were suddenly sticky.

"Here's the torch," said Becky breathlessly. "Christine's just coming."

"No! Don't turn it on!" exclaimed Chris, but he was too late and this time Becky's blood-curdling scream outdid even the one she'd uttered when she'd seen the dead cat. Hazel was lying face down at her feet and jutting out from the middle of her shoulder-blades was a pair of long, wickedly sharp scissors, the kind that were used for cutting wall-paper for the scenery.

For a moment Chris simply stared, and then he had to turn away and grab hold of the curtain. Becky was still screaming, and he could hear voices in the distance as more people came running. The voices started to fade as Chris began to pass out, but he just heard Christine say, "She's dead" to Mike before he lost consciousness.

For the rest of the group it was a moment that would stay in their minds for the rest of their lives. There was Hazel, with the horrible scissors sticking out of her so grotesquely; Christine was bent over her, while Becky stood like a statue, eyes wide with shock, screaming senselessly; and Chris lay collapsed on the floor.

The police were at the scene in a flash. As Claire had guessed, the WPC and two plain-clothes policemen had been sitting in the audience. "We thought that if anything happened it would take place on stage," said the WPC. She sounded distraught. Mike, standing close behind her, knew that he would never be able to forgive himself for insisting on pressing on with the play.

The audience were told that there had been a sudden illness in the cast and their money was refunded as they left, but everyone in the drama group knew that the terrible truth would soon be common knowledge in the town.

Once again, none of them were allowed to leave. This time they stayed together, cast and backstage workers, down in the silent and empty body of the hall.

"One thing's for sure," said Stuart to Steven. "This was no random killing. Whoever murdered Hazel must have known exactly who they were killing, and they were also determined she should die. It isn't like anything else that's happened. No one could imagine Hazel might just as easily have been injured rather than killed. Someone deliberately . . ." His voice petered out as he pictured a faceless figure creeping up behind Hazel and then stabbing her in the back with sufficient force to kill her.

"What interests me," said Steven softly, "is why it was Hazel. What possible grudge could anyone have against her? All she did was help Lynne backstage. She was never very good at anything, and pretty anonymous really. It seems utterly pointless and yet I don't think it was. I think you're right, and this was the first truly deliberate murder. What we have to uncover is the reason why Hazel had to die."

When Detective Sergeant Martin arrived to talk to them, all traces of his previous complacency had gone. He looked worried.

"Listen to me, all of you," he said solemnly. "A dreadful murder has taken place here tonight, and an innocent young girl is dead. One of you knows very well who the killer is, and I'm quite sure that buried deep in your subconscious minds, there must be others of you who have an idea who it is. I'm not saying you're hiding it from us, I credit you with more intelligence than that, but I believe that if you all think hard over every single thing that's happened since the very first incident with the dead cat, you might well come up with some kind of conclusion. If you do, then for heaven's sake come to us with your ideas.

"Don't go gossiping to your friends. Don't try and set a trap or anything along those lines.

Contrary to what you might think from watching television, that is not the way crimes are solved. We catch murderers; that's our job, but we *do* need your help.

"You're all badly shocked and probably can't think straight right now, so I'm not going to keep you. What I want you to do is go away, and start going through everything in your minds. Then, if anything at all strikes you as odd or out of character for someone, please ring the station. One of my team will be there at all times to take the calls. Do I have your word that you'll all co-operate in this? I really believe it's the only way we're going to catch the killer."

Claire, who had been sitting staring at her lap, trying to erase the memory of the scissors sticking up from between Hazel's shoulder-blades, lifted her head. "Does that mean that without our help you haven't got a clue?" she asked.

Detective Sergeant Martin flushed. "Of course not. We have a lot to go on, but you have all been present the whole time. Some of you must have noticed something that didn't quite make sense at the time, even if you didn't realize it then. Your co-operation will make our work easier, that's all I'm saying."

"How will they know who to believe?" Stuart asked James as the police went away. "They very carefully don't mention the fact that one of *us* is the murderer. If they don't know which one, how will they know who to trust?''

"I've no idea," said James. "All I know is that if I had any idea who killed Richard I'd have said so at the time. I wouldn't need a pep talk from Detective Sergeant Martin to go forward with information."

Slowly they all left the hall, well aware that Hazel's death meant the end of the Dorking Future Drama Group.

14

News of the murder was even in some of the national papers the next day. "A Dramatic Death" ran the headline on page three of the *Daily Mail*, while the *Mirror* called it "Teenage Tragedy". There were hints of backstage quarrels and the possibility that Hazel was not the intended victim, but it was all guesswork. None of the drama group had spoken to any reporters, not even local ones, on the advice of the police.

"You can accidentally prejudice a whole inquiry by an incautious word," Detective Sergeant Martin had explained to them, and they agreed immediately to keep silent.

In any case, most of them were too shocked to be able to talk to anyone coherently. Counselling was offered, but none of them used it. They wanted to talk to each other, but the realization that they could be pouring out their feelings to the killer inhibited them. Even now, after two deaths and so many incidents, it was almost impossible to look each other in the eye and accept that the murderer was there among them.

"It's so spooky it doesn't seem real," Suzanne confessed to Emma a week after Hazel's death.

"I know, but it *is* real and we've all got to stay on our guard. Hasn't Steven come up with anything? He's the brainiest member of the group, and he's always talking about it."

"Yes, he talks, but he never gets anywhere." Suzanne hesitated. "Emma, you don't think Steven could be the killer, do you?"

Emma stared at her. "Suzanne! How could you say such a thing about your own brother?"

"Well, whoever's doing all this is probably someone's brother or sister. It's just that as nothing has happened to him, and . . ."

"Look, nothing's happened to you, James or Lynne either, for that matter. Besides, why would Steven want to kill Hazel?"

"Why would anyone want to kill Hazel?" demanded Suzanne.

"I can't imagine, but I do accept someone did. What I'd never accept is that it was *Steven*! You must be daft to suggest it."

Suzanne burst into tears.

"I'm sorry," she sobbed. "I know it was a stupid thing to say, but Mary – the WPC who came to our dress rehearsal – keeps suggesting that perhaps I should think about why it is that Steven and I haven't been hurt, and I can't come up with an answer."

"Nor can the police," said Emma shortly. "That's why they're trying to stir us up. They asked me why I thought you'd escaped it all. I told them my theory about the coffee. That shut them up."

"But I haven't got anything like that I can say for Steven," sniffed Suzanne.

Emma turned to face her friend. "Can you honestly look me in the eye and say that you believe Steven is responsible for all this? Do you think he's capable of killing Richard and Hazel, and nearly murdering Stuart and Claire? Do you?"

"No! No, I don't, but I don't believe any of us are, so that's no comfort because one of us is!" She started to cry even more. "I can't stand it, Emma. It's all so horrible, and no one's getting any closer to finding out who the killer is."

Emma put her arm round Suzanne. "Come on," she said firmly. "We're going to talk to Steven."

As usual on a Saturday afternoon, Steven was studying. At least he was meant to be studying, but inside his History book was a copy of *Henry V*. He was busy learning a speech from it which he thought would make a good audition piece. He shut the History book guiltily as the girls came in.

"Suzanne's at breaking point," Emma announced shortly. "The policewoman who talks to her is suggesting you're the murderer, and she can't cope."

"That's not what I said!" wailed Suzanne, the tears flowing afresh.

Steven sat the two girls down on the edge of his bed and put his arm round his sister. "It's all right, Suzie; I know how you feel. Detective Sergeant Martin keeps saying the same sort of thing about you to me!"

Suzanne looked up at him in surprise. "Me?"

"Yes, and when he goes on and on, sometimes I begin to wonder just a little, the same as you do. That's what they want, Suzie. They've got to get us considering every possibility."

Emma didn't think for one moment that Steven had ever suspected Suzanne; he just wouldn't, but she admired him for telling Suzanne he had. Now Suzanne would stop feeling guilty and would start trusting her brother again.

"At least that's sorted out," she said with satisfaction. "Now perhaps we can all get back to working out who the killer is."

Steven gave her an appreciative smile. "We will. You know, Emma, the way things are going,

Suzanne and I might well need your help soon. Would you be willing to take a bit of a risk to help catch the killer?"

Emma would have done anything for Steven, even cover up for him if he turned out to be the murderer, so she nodded quickly, thrilled that he'd chosen her over Claire. "Of course."

"Great. Suzanne will tell you when the time comes."

"Okay. I'd better get back home now. I'm baby-sitting tonight. Don't forget you're coming round at eight, Suzanne."

Suzanne hiccupped and nodded and Emma ran home in great excitement. At least it was her Steven trusted, and not Claire.

At the same time as all this was going on, Claire was having another fierce argument with her step-father. For once he was sober, but still in his usual bad temper.

"We only let you go to college to get your typing and office skills!" he shouted furiously. "How long do you expect us to go on supporting you? As soon as the year finishes you're finding yourself a job. There are masses of vacancies for filing clerks and office girls. They're on the board at the job centre week after week."

"That's because they're badly paid, dead-end jobs!" Claire shouted back. "I'm not doing it. I refuse to be trapped in a job I loathe just to earn money for you to waste at the pub."

He took a step towards her, his right hand raised, and Claire's mother pushed herself between them. "Stop it, Martin. Leave her alone. She isn't your daughter."

"Too right she isn't. Fine! If I'm not allowed any say in what she does, perhaps her father would like to pay for her to go running off to London to become an actress!"

"I don't want to run off to London; I want to take a Diploma in Drama and then go on to teach it," retorted Claire. "How can that be wrong? I'll be getting qualifications for a good job with prospects."

"You'll be running around for another three years having a good time with your friends while we keep you."

"You don't keep me!" spat Claire, her temper totally out of control. "It's Mum who keeps me by working every night at that horrible food factory. If you were any sort of a man you'd be ashamed to see her so worn out all the time. Don't bother," she added, as he lifted his hand. "I'm going. Dad always said I could go and live with him if I wanted to. Well, now I want to. I'm sorry, Mum," she added with a glance across the room, "but I've had all I can take of him. If I don't get out of here he'll ruin me, just like he's ruined you."

Her mother knew she was right, but contact with Claire's father had been limited since his remarriage and she had no idea how he and his new wife would react to Claire turning up on their doorstep out of the blue.

"Wait until tomorrow, Claire," she begged. "Go round to see him and get him to talk to me about it."

"I'm tired of waiting. Why didn't you throw him out months ago?" she added, glaring at her stepfather.

"I'm her husband and I stay in this house," he shouted. "You go. Your precious dad's welcome to you."

"Please, Claire . . ." began her mother but she was already on her way upstairs to pack.

"Mind you don't get murdered on the way," bellowed her stepfather. "It strikes me life's pretty precarious for members of that infamous drama group of yours."

Back at their home, totally unaware of the sudden change that was about to take place in Claire's life, Steven and Suzanne were talking together.

"Right," said Steven. "We've been through everything. I've written down everyone's names, and as far as possible where they were at the time of each incident. Now, can you come to the same conclusion from what you see on the chart?"

Suzanne studied it carefully. "Not really. The main trouble is that we never know where most of the backstage workers are at any specific moment, although I suppose that's not too important."

"On the contrary, I think it's very important because I believe it's one of the backstage workers who's our killer," said Steven quietly.

"You think James did it?" asked Suzanne.

"No. While James does help backstage he acts as well, and some of the time he's been far too visible to be responsible. I've gone over and over this in my mind, checking and double-checking, and incredible as it's going to seem to you, the one person who comes up as being in a position to do everything is Lynne."

"Lynne?" Suzanne stared at him, totally stupefied.

"Yes. She was late for that first meeting. She could have been collecting the dead cat and then switched it for the toy kitten. She could also have changed the knots on the flats *after* Christine had checked them, because no one would ever wonder what she was doing fiddling around backstage, and – this is important – she told Hazel to keep the coffee table clean. According to Stuart she was also in the changing room before the fire, collecting props from the end where the costume box was.

"But Hazel was her friend, and it was Hazel who died the most horrible death. Lynne would never be able to kill someone with scissors like that. She's a gentle person."

"The Lynne we know is, but the murderer isn't the person we think we know."

"Well, how did she start the fire?" asked Suzanne.

"That would have been quite easy. She was going backwards and forwards to the costume box all the time. She only had to ignite the paper at the bottom just before she left, then slip back and lock the door on Stuart and Claire before she began prompting."

"And nothing has happened to her," said Suzanne slowly.

"That's right, nothing at all. She's never been in any danger. She wasn't on stage when the scenery fell, she wasn't drinking coffee backstage when you and Emma were, and she was never going to be caught in the changing room because the prompt has to be at the side of the stage before the play can begin."

"But why?" asked Suzanne. "There must be some kind of reason in her mind. I accept that it might not seem a logical one to us, but it still has to make sense to her."

Steven nodded. "I know, and so far I haven't been able to come up with anything, but to be honest I don't know much about Lynne as a person. She goes to your school; do you know anything about her home life?"

"Nothing, she's very quiet. In fact, I was surprised she stuck with the drama group. I always thought it was just because she fancied you."

"In other words, we know nothing about her."

"What are we going to do then?" asked Suzanne breathlessly, still trying to come to terms with what Steven was telling her.

"I think she has to be confronted, but not by everyone in the group, just by a few of us. She's plainly sick, and needs help. We'll tell her we understand that. I thought that if you and Emma arranged to meet her, saying you needed to talk about recent events, and I came round a bit later and confronted her with the chart we may be able to get her to admit it all. She doesn't seem a strong character – just a very sick one. Perhaps that's what's behind it all; maybe she resents other more confident members."

"I still can't believe it's her," said Suzanne, but certainly the chart made it look that way.

15

The next day, Steven and Suzanne arranged for Emma to come round. Once they were in the privacy of Suzanne's room they told Emma the conclusion they'd come to. "Stuart agrees with us," Steven added. "I showed him the chart too."

Emma looked as startled as Suzanne had felt. "It doesn't make sense," she complained. "I can see that she *could* have done it, but for the life of me I can't imagine why. She's totally inoffensive, irritatingly so at times."

"Up to a point I agree with you, Emma," said Steven. "I don't know why she should have done it either, but we don't have to know that. Even in a court of law the police don't have to provide their suspect with a motive. In a recent murder trial they came right out and said they hadn't been able to find one. The human mind is too complicated for anyone to fully understand it, and obviously Lynne isn't normal by anyone's standards."

"Meaning what exactly?" asked Emma.

"Meaning that she might well be motivated by some small slight that the rest of us wouldn't even have noticed, but because she's unbalanced it's become an all-consuming passion. She's nurtured the slight until it's grown into a huge insult, one that has to be avenged."

"By killing her own friends?" exclaimed Emma.

"Keep your voice down! Yes, although I doubt she thinks of us as her friends. It's more likely she sees us all as enemies involved in some kind of conspiracy against her."

Emma shook her head in disbelief. "Have you read lots of books on psychology or something? I mean, this is just too way out for me. Maybe it is Lynne, and if it is then obviously she's mad, but as for all the rest, you've lost me."

"Sorry, I suppose I do go on a bit, but the human mind fascinates me."

"So what do we do?" asked Emma practically.

Suzanne leant forward. "Steven thought that one of us should ring Lynne up and suggest a meeting. If we make out that we think we know who the murderer is and want her help in catching them, she shouldn't make any trouble."

Emma frowned. "I'd have thought she'd be highly suspicious."

"No," said Steven. "She must be feeling really confident by now. The police don't seem interested in her, no one in the group has ever suggested it was her . . ."

"I remember her flying to her own defence for no obvious reason that night we were at James's house," said Emma. "She got very worked up."

"Yes, I'd forgotten that!" agreed Suzanne. "She ended up crying, didn't she?"

"Probably. Anyway, go on."

"Yes, right. Well, we meet up with her and start chatting, suggesting different people in the group that we think it is, leading her on to make some suggestions of her own until she's thoroughly off guard, and then Steven will join us and confront her with the chart."

"And then?" asked Emma.

Steven and Suzanne looked at her, puzzled.

"What's she meant to do? Break down and confess like on television, I suppose. Well, what if she doesn't? What if she brazens it out and says we're the ones who are mad and she's going to complain to her parents? We'll look pretty stupid then. Or, if she's as mad as Steven thinks, she could go totally off-the-wall and attack us."

"That's what I'm hoping!" said Steven excitedly. "I believe that once she's cornered she'll show her true colours and then we've got her. I'm going to take a tape recorder along in my pocket and keep it running the whole time. If she tries anything, the three of us can easily overpower her, and the tape will record every word she utters for the police."

"I don't think it will work," said Emma flatly. "She's kept her nerve this far. The three of us aren't the law or anything. We're no threat at all."

"She might not confess, if it weren't for the fact that I'm going to tell a small fib. I'm going to say that she was seen turning the key on the changing room door just before Claire and Stuart were trapped."

"Seen by whom?" demanded Emma.

"By Hazel. I shall say that Hazel was worried by what she'd seen and told me. It's quite likely Hazel did know something. Perhaps the talk by Detective Sergeant Martin made her go over some tiny incident until it made a dreadful kind of sense, but instead of going to the police she went to the person she'd seen – her friend Lynne. That's almost certainly why Hazel had to die. What Lynne won't know is that Hazel never spoke to anyone else."

"Clever!" agreed Emma approvingly. "Even if that wasn't the incident Hazel saw, she *could* have seen Lynne then. They were both backstage at the same time."

"Right! Now, do you think it will work and are you willing to help us?"

"Why not go to the police and tell them all this?" asked Emma.

"Because they'll say we haven't any proof – which we haven't – and then start ferreting around asking questions which will put her on her guard. I believe that if we don't do this, Lynne's going to get away with it."

Suzanne watched breathlessly as Emma's face reflected her indecision, but at last she nodded. "Right, count me in. When's Suzanne going to ring Lynne?"

"I'd hoped you'd do it," said Steven. "The group knows that Suzanne and I have been doing some amateur detective work and I think Suzanne calling her might arouse her suspicions. If you ring, saying it's something you and Suzie have worked out together, she's far more likely to feel safe and agree to help you."

"Where shall we meet her?" asked Suzanne.

"How about the rehearsal hall?" suggested Emma quickly. "That will add atmosphere to the confrontation. Surrounded by all those memories, isn't she more likely to crack?"

"But we can't get in any more; it's kept locked," said Steven.

"We could use that small window backstage. The one we use when we're late for rehearsals and Mike's locked the doors against us!"

"Great idea. I think we should do this as soon as

possible. How about trying for tonight? No one uses the social hall on a Sunday night."

"All right," agreed Emma. "About what time?"

"Let's see; we usually finish tea by six, then you and Suzanne have to meet up and walk to the hall so probably seven o'clock would be best. I'll give you thirty minutes' start, then come along, slip in through the window and join you. Where will you be, do you think? In the hall itself?"

"On the stage might be best," said Suzanne, beginning to feel a rising excitement herself. "The set's still up as far as I know. If we can point to the actual spot where Richard died, surely that would have a lot of impact."

"I agree," said Emma. "On the stage, face to face – very dramatic."

"Just make sure you get her completely off-guard. The success of all this depends on the element of surprise, which I shall supply with my sudden appearance from the wings."

"You could bring Stuart too, for back-up," Emma suggested. "I think we'd feel safer if there were two of you. Lynne's quite well-built and I don't fancy my chances with her in a physical tussle."

"I'm hoping there won't be too much of one; but perhaps Stuart would be a good idea," Steven agreed.

"Right. I'll ring Lynne as soon as I get back, and then let you know if she's agreed to meet us," said

Emma. "My mother would go crazy if she knew what I was doing."

"Won't she ask where you're going?" said Suzanne.

"Yes, but I'll say I'll be at your place. That's where I usually go; she'll hardly be suspicious of that!"

"I didn't think she was going to agree," said Suzanne to Steven, after she'd gone.

"I wasn't sure, but now there are four of us who think the same way, and the chart doesn't show any other obvious suspect so I really think we've got it cracked."

"You won't be far behind us, will you?" said Suzanne nervously.

"Of course not. If you like, Stuart and I will only wait fifteen minutes after you set off before following."

"That would be better. We might find it difficult to keep her talking for longer than that. At least after tonight it will all be over," she added.

"Providing she agrees to the meeting," said Steven. "We'll have to keep our fingers crossed that Emma's convincing enough over the phone."

"It's on!" said Emma half an hour later, her voice tight with a mixture of fear and excitement over the telephone. "Lynne's agreed to meet us. The only problem is that I have to look after Paula until a quarter to seven, so you'd better come to my house, Suzie, and we'll go on from there. I've told Mum we're going to the cinema."

"Fine. Emma, are you nervous?"

"Of course I'm nervous; in fact I'm petrified, but I only have to think about Richard and Hazel and I get furious instead. She can't be allowed to get away with it."

"So you're sure Steven's right?"

"It all makes sense. There's only the motive business, but again he was right there. The motive probably won't mean anything to us when it does come out. I'll have to go now," she added, dropping her voice, "Paula's here with a book. I've promised to read to her. Wrap up well tonight, it will be freezing in the hall. See you soon."

"See you," echoed Suzanne, putting down the phone. She turned to her brother. "Lynne accepted. I'm going round to Emma's and then we'll go on to the hall together."

"So Lynne wasn't suspicious?"

"It doesn't seem like it. You don't think we should tell the police what we're doing, do you?"

"Absolutely not," said Steven firmly. "This is something we have to sort out for ourselves. There's a phone outside the hall. I'll call them as soon as there's anything to tell and hand the tape recorder over at the same time. Don't worry, Suzanne, I wouldn't let any harm come to you."

"It's only that they warned us against this," Suzanne murmured.

"They'll be grateful enough when we hand them the murderer before the night's finished," said Steven.

"I still can't believe it was Lynne," muttered Suzanne, walking upstairs to her room.

16

"You're a bit early," said Emma when she opened the front door to Suzanne. "I hope Lynne will be there."

"If not we'll just have to hang around until she arrives. That won't matter, and I'll be warm enough. I took your advice about wrapping up."

Both of the girls had boots on over their leggings and wore gloves and scarves to keep out the biting east wind. They knew they didn't look fashionable, but at that particular moment they had more important things on their minds.

Sure enough, when they got to the hall there was no sign of Lynne. "She'll come along the main road," said Suzanne. "We'd better wait by the side door; that way we'll see her before she sees us."

"What difference will that make?" asked Emma

with a grin, but she humoured Suzanne, who was feeling decidedly nervous about what lay ahead.

They stood by the door for a moment, huddled close to the building to keep out of the wind. Suzanne leant back and nearly fell inside as the door swung gently open. "It isn't locked!" she exclaimed.

Emma narrowed her eyes. "That's very odd. The caretaker's been extra vigilant since the murders. He knows the police keep popping round. I'd have thought he'd be more careful."

"Perhaps Lynne's already in there," suggested Suzanne, her voice shaking a little. "Suppose she still has her key?"

"It's more likely she had a spare cut when she was in charge of the backstage workers. That would have made it easy for her to come and go as she pleased," said Emma.

"If she's already in there, does that mean she's suspicious of us?" Suzanne asked anxiously.

"I don't suppose so."

"Then why didn't she tell you she had a key?"

Emma hesitated. "Probably because I didn't ask. Neither did I say we'd all climb in through the window. She must have thought I expected her to have a key."

"It could be a trap," said Suzanne, staring through the gap in the doorway and into the darkness beyond.

"If it is, it's a bit of an obvious one."

"But she's early!" protested Suzanne.

"So are we. That isn't a crime. Come on, let's go in. I'm freezing out here."

Suzanne hesitated. Something didn't feel right and she'd wanted to meet up with Lynne outside, to be sure that she was friendly and unsuspicious before going inside the building with her. "I'm not sure we should, Emma."

"Why ever not?"

"Because it might not be Lynne in there. Suppose it's the police?"

"If it's the police we'll say we're looking for a purse I lost and go straight out again."

"Then what happens to Lynne?"

Emma grabbed hold of her arm. "For heaven's sake, Suzanne! I'm going in. Are you coming with me or not?"

There was no way Suzanne was going to let her friend leave her alone outside and she gave a small squeak of discomfort. "Let go of me! Of course I'm coming, I'm just not in such a rush to get killed as you are."

"No one's going to get killed. Your brother will make sure of that. Let's go."

They stepped cautiously into the dingy entrance hall. It was unlit, which Suzanne thought odd if Lynne was already inside, and the door that led backstage was tightly closed. "I don't think we're expected," said Suzanne.

Emma tripped against the step by the door and bent down to rub her ankle. "Ouch! That hurt! Mind how you go, Suzanne. Put the lights on; the switch is just round the corner."

Suzanne moved past her friend, reaching round and up the wall, groping for the light switch. Her fingers quickly found it and she flicked it down. Nothing happened. The lights stayed off.

"It's not working!" she hissed back to Emma.

"Blast! Never mind, there's a back-up switch in the prompt corner. We'll have to find our way there."

"But where's Lynne?" asked Suzanne in bewilderment. "Surely she's not hiding in the dark? Why hasn't she come to help us?"

"I don't know." Emma was beginning to sound cross and frightened as well. "Let's call her. Lynne! Lynne, are you there?"

There was no answer. The darkness remained resolutely silent. Suzanne and Emma stood totally still, listening for the sound of movement or even breathing, but there was nothing.

"It's as though we're alone," whispered Suzanne.

"What did you say?" Emma whispered back, reaching up for the back-up light switch.

"I said it's as though we're alone."

The lights suddenly illuminated the stage and at the same time Suzanne felt something hard hit her between the shoulder-blades so that she skidded onto the stage and fell onto the floor boards, skinning her hands and tearing the knees of her leggings as she did so.

"Emma, look out!" she screamed, lifting her head, but the sudden brilliance of the stage lighting had temporarily blinded her and it was only at the last moment that she saw the heavy piece of wood come crashing down towards her. She instinctively raised her arm, which took the full force of the blow. There was the sound of a bone cracking, and a dreadful pain shot up her forearm, making her want to retch.

"Emma, run!" she called. "There's someone here."

"No there isn't," said Emma in a cold voice. "There's just you and me."

For a moment, Suzanne wondered if she'd hit her head and been concussed without knowing it. "Run!" she repeated through tears of pain. "I've been hit. Get help."

"I'm afraid I've no intention of getting help," said Emma, walking calmly in front of the injured Suzanne. "You see, I've brought you here to kill you."

Suzanne stared up at her friend. Emma looked the same. Her short dark hair was still shiny and beautifully cut; her brown eyes were just as bright, possibly brighter than usual, all of which made the words she was uttering even more incomprehensible.

"Kill me?" she repeated stupidly.

"Yes. It was you I was after all along. Right from the start, you were the one I was working up to, but I had to wait. If I'd hurried, done it too soon, someone might have guessed. They won't now. Thanks to your clever brother it will be Lynne who takes the blame for your death, along with all the others. You and I were just pawns in his game of amateur detectives. A game which I shall say went horribly wrong when I'm finally able to give a coherent account of the events here tonight to the police."

"Emma, you can't mean it. This is a joke, isn't it? Some kind of silly joke."

"Does the pain in your arm feel like a joke?"

It didn't. The pain was like nothing Suzanne had ever experienced before, and her fingers were already swelling and going numb. She couldn't stop the tears from running down her face, and despite her warm clothing she was shivering as if she were caught in a blizzard.

"But Emma, why?" she asked pitifully. "We've been best friends for years."

"I went off you," said Emma flatly. "I only stayed your friend because I wanted to be close to Steven. I've hated you for ages, if you must know."

"You can't have done!" cried Suzanne. She felt as though she was trapped in a nightmare, the kind where everything in life is turned upside down, but the pain in her arm told her this was no nightmare. This was reality.

"I'm afraid I have. You were easy to hate. You see, you had everything that I've ever wanted but couldn't get. You had a nice home, happy, loving parents and an adoring older brother who protected you from everything. If you came bottom in a Maths test he'd give up a free evening to help you understand where you'd gone wrong. When you failed to make the school hockey team he coached you in the back garden until you were so good you took my place. And every summer the four of you went off like one of those awful families in the adverts, smiling and cheerful, for your two-week holiday in the sun. It all made me feel like chucking up."

Suzanne's head was spinning and she was having trouble getting her thoughts together but she knew that if she could only keep Emma talking a little longer, Steven and Stuart would be there. Emma didn't know he'd decided to follow after fifteen minutes. They'd hung around outside for quite some time, so it wouldn't be long before the boys arrived.

"You had holidays, Emma," she protested. "And your parents were happy once."

"No they weren't; they always argued and fought in private. Then, after the divorce, it was worse. For a while Mum and I were close, but once David and his horrible brat Paula arrived I was pushed right out. All I was good for was babysitting and reading to her. They seemed to forget I had a life of my own to live."

"But what difference will killing me make to your life?" asked Suzanne, trying desperately to make some kind of sense out of Emma's string of complaints.

"Can't you even see that? You really are dim. It will make your precious brother turn to me for comfort, of course. He's been seeing me like a second sister instead of a potential girlfriend for the past year, and that's really what made me think of this plan. I thought, why should I be the *second* sister? I'll be the first. With you gone, I'll be his only sister, won't I? I was always better at logical thinking than you, Suzanne."

Suzanne couldn't believe that it was Emma talking: her best friend, the person she'd always thought she knew best in the world after her family. Here she was, babbling total nonsense and then calling it logic, but Suzanne wasn't going to argue. She had to keep Emma relaxed.

"How did you get the door unlocked?" she asked weakly.

"Hazel had a spare key cut for me. She did quite

a lot of things for me, because I was the only one who took the trouble to be nice to her. She was lonely too. I knew how that felt and deliberately let her think I was her friend. She put the turps in your coffee mug; I said it was just a joke. The trouble was she put it in the wrong one, but in the end that worked out for the best."

"And I suppose you never really rang Lynne, asking her to meet us here?"

"Correct! I never asked her to meet us here, and furthermore I rang your brother after you'd left and told him Lynne had put the meeting back an hour, so I'm afraid he and Stuart won't be charging in like the cavalry to rescue you in the nick of time."

At this, Suzanne gave a wail of frustration. Emma moved closer to her. "I thought that might give you something to think about. You've been playing for time, haven't you? Trying to keep me talking until the boys arrived, but they're not coming. By the time they do get here you'll be dead and the police will go and arrest Lynne."

"She might have an alibi for tonight!" said Suzanne with a spark of rebellion.

"Afraid not. You see, I did call her, but pretending to be you. I asked her to meet me at the bottom of the field by Hatchett's Farm. No one ever goes there. She'll have no witnesses of her trip and I shall say she ran off there after she'd killed you. Now, time for some action, I think."

17

Suzanne looked up at Emma's face. It was blood-less except for two spots of hectic colour on her cheeks. Emma was reaching into the back pocket of her jacket and as Suzanne watched, she brought out a long, red-handled kitchen knife which glinted horribly in the stage lights.

"I've thought and thought about how to kill you," said Emma in a chatty voice. "There were so many options, but in the end I decided the most satisfying way to do it would be to cut your throat. I wore the gloves because of fingerprints, not to keep out the cold as you thought."

"No!" Although the pain was making it difficult for Suzanne to concentrate, she began to edge backwards, trying to get nearer the false door they'd used in the play. Adrenalin began to flood through her body, helping to dull the pain and sharpen her wits.

"Is there anything else you want to know before you die?" Emma asked her. "I think I've been pretty clever. I don't mind telling you about it."

"Did you mean the other two to die?" Suzanne asked, grateful for the extra time Emma's mad vanity was giving her.

"Not Richard, no; I didn't have anything against him, but I had to keep the accidents going and he was unlucky. Hazel was different. She had to be killed. She was going to the police about the pranks she'd helped me play with the coffee and the dead cat. Luckily she didn't believe I was the killer; she just felt it her duty to say what she knew. She also thought it was her duty to tell me first, probably hoping I'd own up so that my 'jokes' didn't get in the way of the murder enquiry, so I murdered her before she could speak to the police after the first performance."

"Emma, this isn't right," said Suzanne, still edging slowly backwards. "You're not an evil person, you're sick. You need help, and I promise I'll make sure you get it. Just stop now, let me go, and everything will be all right."

Emma sneered at her. "Do you think I'm simple or something? Of course everything won't be 'all right' if I let you go. But it will be all right if I kill you. I'll be the weeping heroine who grappled with Lynne and tried to save you – I can inflict a few injuries on myself to make that convincing – and I'll be Steven's only sister. We'll support each other at the funeral, talking about the good old days all the time, remembering your sweet little ways and the fun we had together! He won't have time for Claire once he's grieving for you. She's never been your friend, she won't be able to talk to him about days gone by. Now stop inching your way backwards, Suzanne, and keep still for me. It will be much easier if you don't put up a fight."

"Easier for you, you mean," said Suzanne, wishing that everything didn't keep going misty and that the pain from her arm wasn't spreading so relentlessly through her shoulder and up the side of her neck.

Emma laughed. It was a bitter, humourless sound. "I don't mind if you struggle, it will make it all the more satisfying for me. It's you I'm thinking of. And Steven," she added in a gentler tone. "It would be awful for him to arrive here and see a trail of your blood all over the stage. Much better to stay in one place and let me do it cleanly."

"I'd hardly have sat here and let Lynne slaughter me like a pig on a farm," Suzanne pointed out.

"Now that is logical thinking. However, I shall say that Lynne came at you from behind, because I shall actually slit your throat from behind. I think I might find it difficult to do it while looking into your eyes."

"Emma, please!" Suzanne begged as the other girl advanced towards her. "I've always liked you. Think of how we've helped each other at school, and the times we've giggled about some of the other girls. And think of what Steven will do when you're caught, because you will be caught one day."

Emma was like a machine. She kept advancing, upraised piece of wood in her left hand in case Suzanne found the strength to get up and try to escape, knife held firmly in her right hand, blade away from her own body. "He'll never know, because I'll never be caught. They'll arrest Lynne and the killings will stop. Everything I did was leading up to this moment. Your death had to be one of a series; that way the police would never look for someone with a motive for killing *you*. They'd just see you as a victim of a serial killer."

"Please, Emma, don't kill me!" Suzanne begged her. "I don't want to die. It isn't fair. I've never hurt you. I've never done anything to you."

"Life isn't fair," hissed Emma through clenched teeth. "Perhaps you've never meant to hurt me, but you have with your sickly happiness."

"Your mother loves you, and so does your step-father and . . ."

"You don't know anything about him!" screamed

Emma, her face contorting into a hideous travesty of its usual expression. "He's hateful, vile. He watches me all the time. I can't get away from his beastly prying eyes and I know what he's thinking, even if he never says. Oh yes, I know all about him."

"You're mad!" exclaimed Suzanne.

For a moment the two girls stared at each other, and then with a hiss of rage Emma brought the wood crashing down on Suzanne's good hand. For a moment she didn't feel anything, and then the pain hit her and she screamed at the top of her voice.

"That's right, scream!" shouted Emma. "Scream as loud as you can. Beg for your life, plead with me, make as much noise as it's possible for a human being to make. I don't care. I'll listen, and when you've exhausted yourself, I'll finish you off. Come on, Suzanne, let me hear you scream. There isn't anyone else around, I'm afraid, but I'll make a good audience for your final performance."

Suzanne shut her mouth tightly. She wasn't going to scream any more. She wouldn't give Emma the final satisfaction her mad, tortured soul craved. Instead she shut her eyes and shuffled round so that her back was towards her would-be killer.

"I see. You want it over, do you?" said Emma, disappointment tinging her voice. "Well, I can't make you scream so I suppose I'll just have to get on with it."

"Could you wait a moment?" asked a familiar voice. "I haven't got a very good view from here," and as both Emma and Suzanne turned their heads in amazement, Claire sauntered on to the stage.

It would have been difficult to know which of the two girls was most surprised by her arrival. Suzanne whimpered and tried to move towards her, while Emma simply gaped. Her mouth opened in astonishment, but she still kept a firm grip on both the wood and the knife.

"Stay where you are!" she snarled as she began to recover from the shock. "Don't move any nearer or I'll kill you too."

Claire raised her eyebrows. "And how would you explain that scenario when our bodies were discovered? The police might well believe that you couldn't stop Lynne killing Suzanne, but me too? I think that would stretch their imagination a little."

"I'll take that chance," said Emma, her eyes darting around, searching the shadows for other unexpected arrivals.

"There's no one else here," said Claire. "Only me. Now, where do you think I should stand in order to get the best view of the murder?"

If Suzanne hadn't been speechless with the pain from her left arm and right hand she would have screamed at Claire. How could she be so callous?

she wondered despairingly. Why didn't she just rush at Emma?

Claire had considered that, and she'd also earlier considered trying to slip out of the building unseen and telephoning the police, but Emma's increasing determination to slit Suzanne's throat had forced her to show herself instead. For the first time she thanked her father and stepmother for being out when she'd arrived at their home unexpectedly. The hall was the one place where she knew she could shelter for the night quite safely.

"How did you get in?" asked Emma.

"Through the window, of course. Shall I stand downstage left? I could see you rather well from there."

Emma's mind began to race out of control. She had planned the evening so carefully, right down to the finest detail. Now Claire, Claire whom she already hated because of Steven, had turned up to spoil it all and Emma didn't know what to do about it.

"You can't watch," she said fiercely. "This isn't a play. If you watched, you'd be an accessory to murder," she pointed out.

Claire drew in a quick breath. She'd hoped that sheer astonishment would confuse Emma so much that she'd go to pieces, but it didn't seem to be happening. True, she had moved away from Suzanne, and for the moment it didn't look as though she was going to kill her within the next few seconds, but none of her fanatical determination had disappeared. She was still thinking well within her own framework of twisted logic.

"I suppose it would make me an accessory," Claire conceded. "Mind you, I'd say that I was too frightened to stop you."

"And I'd say we were in it together," said Emma, eyes ablaze with the thrill of this new idea. "Yes, I'd say we'd acted as a pair right from the start. You because you were jealous of Becky, and me because . . ."

"Why?" asked Claire gently. "Why have you done it all?"

"I've been through all that! You've been listening, you already know."

"I heard the words," said Claire, "but I didn't understand."

Emma glanced at Suzanne, saw that she was huddled in a motionless heap, and turned back to Claire. "No, I don't suppose you did, because you aren't me. You haven't lost your father to another woman, then your mother's love to another man, and had to spend half your days looking after some beastly five-year-old that everyone dotes on, while your stepfather never stops watching you."

"Perhaps he was just trying to see if you were happy," suggested Claire.

"No he wasn't! He was spying on me!" She moved towards Suzanne.

"I'm so sorry," said Claire in a sarcastic tone.

"You don't sound it. But then, you never think about anyone but yourself, do you? Sharp-tongued, self-contained Claire. I can't imagine what Steven sees in you."

"Why should I think about anyone but myself? As you know, no one else will think about me if I don't. My father left home too. I don't blame him, my mother nagged him from dawn to dusk, but it's a pity he didn't think about me before he took off. Later, Mum met someone else, and I was quite pleased, until they got married. Then the boot was really on the other foot. After that, he nagged *her* all the time, and when he wasn't going on at her he was off down the pub drinking away all the money, including the maintenance Dad was paying for me. You're quite right; I don't feel sorry for you because I think you've had it pretty easy compared with me."

"Suzanne's had it easier than both of us," said Emma, clearly thrown by Claire's unexpected revelations.

"And that means she has to die?" Claire managed to sound slightly amused, which once again confused Emma, who was finding it difficult to hold on to the festering fury that had sustained her for so long.

"Yes, because then I can take her place," she explained.

Claire nodded, as though that made perfect sense. "Move into her home, wear her clothes, that kind of thing?"

"No, I don't mean literally! Can't you see! When she's dead the people who loved her will love me instead, and only me. I'll come first with people for once, instead of second or third. I want to be first. It's my turn." Her voice was rising again and her eyes glittering.

"I find it quite hard to imagine that Steven will love you more than anyone else after you've killed his sister, but if you're willing to take that chance you'd better go ahead," said Claire.

All the time she'd been talking she'd also been looking around her for a weapon, and by walking slowly down front, where she'd claimed she'd have the best view of the murder, she was now within touching distance of the small chair used by the prompter. "Right," she said brightly. "I'm in position, let murder commence."

18

While the conversation between Emma and Claire had been going on, Suzanne had drifted in and out of consciousness. Now and again one or two words would penetrate her mind, but Claire's final sentence was so bizarre that Suzanne decided the pain must be making her brain play tricks on her.

As Claire had planned, Emma found it bizarre too. She watched Claire suspiciously, waiting for her to make a run for it or rush towards her, but Claire didn't move. She simply stood downstage with an expectant, interested expression on her face, waiting, as she'd said, for the murder to commence.

Emma didn't know what to do. Never, in any of her sick and twisted plans, had she considered committing a murder in front of a witness. It wasn't something that she'd prepared for, and as a result she no longer knew how to proceed. She knew that it wasn't possible, that a witness meant discovery and imprisonment, but she had no idea how to get rid of Claire.

"You must be out of your mind!" she blurted out. "How can you stand there and watch? That's really sick."

"Not as sick as killing people," said Claire placidly.

"But I've got a reason. You shouldn't be here. You're not part of the plan."

"Sorry about that. What am I supposed to do? Vanish?"

Emma shook her head. "No, I suppose you'll have to die too, but you're right about that making it difficult for me. I think I'll have to hurt myself badly as well. I'll make it look as though Lynne left us all for dead."

Claire had reasoned that eventually this was what Emma would decide to do, which was why she was standing by the chair, but guessing it was coming and actually hearing the words were two very different things. Now it was Claire's turn to feel her scalp prickle with terror and a thin line of sweat beaded her top lip while her mouth turned dry.

"Which of us dies first?" she asked in a cracked voice.

"It has to be you," said Emma. "Suzanne's too badly hurt to cause me any trouble, but you might attack me while I kill her."

"Yes, I might."

Emma hesitated. "I'm sorry. I never meant you to get involved, especially with all your problems and things. It doesn't seem right."

"It isn't right to kill anyone. Don't let my personal problems trouble you," retorted Claire.

Behind Emma, Suzanne uttered a groan of pain, and the sound galvanized Emma into action. Without warning she rushed towards Claire, striking out wildly with the piece of wood and jabbing forward with the knife at the same time.

Claire ducked, swayed away from the knife, took two steps back and grabbed hold of the back of the chair, then held it in front of her like a shield.

With a howl of rage, Emma smashed her piece of wood against the chair. The wood she was holding had been cut off the end of one of the heavy supporting struts and was far stronger than the flimsy chair Claire was using to protect herself. Immediately the two made contact, the leg of the chair snapped off.

Claire screamed then jabbed the chair forward, hoping the jagged edge of the broken leg might stab Emma, but Emma leapt out of the way and began to laugh.

"You don't stand a chance, Claire. I'm stronger

than you! I'm stronger than anyone! Why not give in?"

Breathing heavily, Claire continued to jab the chair at Emma as she circled around until she was between the demented teenager and Suzanne. It was frightening even to look at Emma now. Her hair was sticking to her head and her face seemed to have fallen in, while her eyes were huge and dark in their sockets. She no longer looked like the girl they'd all known. She looked what she was: totally deranged.

"You can't win! You can't win!" shrieked Emma, raining blows down on the chair with the piece of wood, her arm rising and falling in a powerful frenzy. The chair quickly splintered into pieces until all Claire was left holding was the runged back.

Emma laughed, swung her piece of wood sideways and tore Claire's last shred of protection from her hands, catching her a sickening blow across the knuckles as she did it. Now it was Claire's turn to cry tears of pain. She tried to control them but failed, which meant that at this vital moment her vision was blurred.

Frantically she dashed into the wings, deliberately tangling herself up in the thick velvet curtain. Although it provided temporary protection, it was a mistake, and Claire knew that as soon as she'd done it. It would cushion her from the knife for a short time, but it would also hold her fast. As Emma slashed at the curtain with her knife and the material ripped, Claire realized that in a very few seconds it would be her body that the knife was striking.

She twisted and turned, trying to work her way free, but the curtain had many heavy folds and clung to her, so that the more she struggled the more she got caught up. Emma's face was very close to hers now, and her lip was pulled back over her top teeth in a ghastly parody of a smile.

"It's a pity there's no one here to see this death scene," she snarled, slashing at the curtain again. "I should think it looks very effective."

"Stop it!" shouted Claire. "This is stupid. You'll never get away with it, Emma. Not now. The moment I heard you talking to Suzanne it was all over. Can't you understand that? No one will believe Lynne managed to kill two of us and . . ." She screamed as the edge of the knife cut through the last layer of the material and pierced the skin of her left arm.

"I think this was meant to happen!" gasped Emma, her own breathing ragged after the struggle. "Now you won't even be around for Steven, so he'll have to turn to me. Yes, fate was on my side for once." She slashed again, and another burning pain assailed Claire.

Claire knew that her only hope was Suzanne,

but when she saw that Suzanne still hadn't moved an inch she finally accepted that despite her best efforts, she too was going to die.

Emma saw the change of expression in Claire's eyes, saw the moment of ultimate terror grip her, and laughed. "That's right, Claire! This is it! This is your last appearance on stage!"

Claire closed her eyes, and braced herself for the final cut of the knife, but suddenly there was a crashing sound as the doors into the hall were flung open, then footsteps pounded up the stairs and two figures burst into the spotlight.

Startled, Emma turned and found herself face to face with the one person who mattered to her, the person she'd done everything for, Steven. He was staring at the scene in front of him in disbelief, and his shock and disgust were clear for her to see.

It was the disgust that was her undoing. She wanted him to love her, to respect her and be her friend, not look at her with loathing. Quickly she dropped the knife and tried to smile at him. She had no idea how terrifying the sight of that smile was to Steven and Stuart.

"We're just rehearsing," she said in a strange, high voice filled with false enthusiasm. "I've had this great idea for a murder play, and Claire and Suzanne have kindly said they'd go through it with me. We wanted to see if the actual killings would work. You can come out now, Claire," she added in an off-hand tone. "I think everything seems okay."

Claire, her heart hammering as though it was going to burst, simply collapsed inside the curtain, her knees buckling as the shock and relief hit her at the same time.

"She's mad," whispered Stuart, his feet unable to move him the spot. "We must call the police."

"Don't go yet," Steven whispered back. "She's still got the wood. I'll keep her talking. You try to see how Suzanne is."

"How did it look?" Emma continued, edging away from the whimpering Claire.

"Very good," replied Steven warmly. "Christine never wrote anything as convincing as that." If ever he needed proof that he was going to make it as an actor, this was it, he thought to himself, because despite the dreadful sight before him his voice sounded genuinely enthusiastic.

Emma clapped her hands together like a little girl, and as she did so the piece of wood fell to the stage with a loud thud. Steven concentrated hard on ignoring it; he knew that he must keep up eye contact with Emma if Claire and Suzanne were to escape alive.

"I knew it! You see, I am good at something."

"You're good at lots of things," he assured her. "You've been a very good friend to Suzanne, and . . ."

"I don't want to be a good friend to Suzanne," she snapped, her voice turning harsh again. "I want to be *your* friend."

"You are," he said quickly. "You're the nicest girl I've ever met."

"Then why didn't you ask me to the party?" she demanded, her eyes narrowing suspiciously.

Steven heard Suzanne give a small moan as Stuart bent over her, and saw how Emma's eyes darted towards her, burning with hatred. He tried to martial his thoughts, to think of an answer that would satisfy her.

"To be honest, Emma, I didn't think I was good enough for you. You're so clever and attractive, and you never seemed interested in me in that way. I thought you only liked me as a brother." He waited uncertainly, but this was the best thing he could have said because now Emma was both proud and taken aback.

"I thought you only liked me as a sister; a *second* sister," she said in happy amazement.

"If only you'd told me, Emma!" said Steven, taking a cautious step towards her.

"Then you didn't really like Claire?"

"No, she was definitely second best."

"But you loved Suzanne more than me, didn't you?"

Steven swallowed hard. He could see that Stuart was now moving off the stage, presumably to call the police and an ambulance. He knew that was the right decision for Stuart, but he still had to keep Emma calm.

"Suzanne's all right as sisters go, but she can be a bit of a nuisance sometimes, the way she tags along. I only ever let her because it meant I could see more of you."

"Really?" Emma's face lit up, and she ran towards him. "That's wonderful, Steven! So I do come first with you! It wasn't Suzanne and it wasn't Claire; it was me all the time!"

"It was you all the time, Emma," he told her softly.

Then, to his disbelief, Emma came right up to him and rested her head against his chest. "Hug me, Steven," she said, her voice once again like a little girl's. "Hold me tight. You could sing to me. Sing me a lullaby."

Steven's brain froze. He couldn't think of a single lullaby. He had no idea what to sing instead, or how to make himself put his arms round this deranged figure snuggled up against him, crooning to herself, but he knew that he must do something. She was quiet now, but she could easily change, and he had to keep her quiet until the police arrived.

Slowly he forced his arms round her, feeling her tense body slacken a little in the safety of his embrace. For a moment a shaft of pity cut through his disgust and he wondered what it was that had turned the happy outgoing girl he'd once known into this mad creature he was holding. Taking a deep breath he began to sing the only song he knew from appearing in his school's production of *West Side Story*. It was called, "One Hand, One Heart" and as he sang, Emma closed her eyes in ecstasy.

19

When the police and ambulancemen arrived, Emma was still standing in Steven's embrace, and he was singing the same song only very quietly, because he could tell that Emma's mind had drifted off into a world of her own, where everything was exactly as she had planned it.

As two policemen and a policewoman gently disengaged Emma from Steven her eyes opened and she stared at them in bewilderment. "What's the matter?" she asked plaintively. "Why have I got to leave?"

"Your mother wants to see you," said the policewoman softly. "Come along; we'll take you to her."

"Is Paula with her?" Emma sounded agitated again.

"She's quite alone," one of the policemen said truthfully, still trying to make sense of the bizarre scene they were witnessing.

"All right then, I'll come," agreed Emma, seeming to think she had a choice in the matter, and they began to lead her away. At the stage exit she glanced back over her shoulder. "Will you come round to see me tonight?" she asked, in her normal voice.

"Of course," Steven replied evenly.

"We can go out for a burger and coke. Suzanne used to like burgers and cokes. Do you remember the times the three of us went out together?"

"Yes," said Steven, and the lump in his throat was so large he had trouble speaking clearly. "I'll always remember," he assured her.

Emma smiled. "I thought you would." And then she was gone.

It was the sound of Suzanne groaning that jerked Steven back to an awareness of what had happened. He dashed over to her, and found an ambulance-man already there.

"She's suffered a couple of bad breaks to her arm," he said in a low voice. "We'll get a stretcher. Shock and pain are a dangerous combination. Put your jacket round her until we get the blankets here."

Steven took off his leather jacket and went to wrap it round her, but Suzanne shook her head.

"No, it will hurt my arm. Is Claire all right? She saved my life."

"I haven't checked yet. Is the pain terrible, Suzie? I expect you'll get given something for it in a minute."

She tried to keep her eyes open, exhausted by the whole nightmare experience. "It was worse earlier. Now it's going numb. Thank heavens you got here when you did."

"It was thanks to Lynne," said Steven. "I'll tell you about it when you're better." He took hold of her uninjured hand. "I'm sorry, Suzie. This was all my fault."

"It doesn't matter. It's over now," she said. Then the ambulancemen returned, wrapping her carefully in blankets before hurrying her out into the ambulance. Stuart went with them. As he gazed down at Suzanne, he realized that they'd come close to losing her and Claire as well as Richard and Hazel.

Once his sister had been taken away, Steven went across to where a doctor was attending Claire. He'd been fetched by the police from his home just over the road, and had quickly staunched the bleeding from her upper arm, where the final knife blow had struck.

"This young lady's going to need quite a few stitches in her wounds," he told Steven. "If I take her in my car, can you sit in the back with her?"

Steven nodded, silenced by Claire's terrible pallor and the knowledge that she too was the victim of his own conviction that he knew more than the police about the crimes within the drama group. It was a sobering thought.

Claire leant on his arm as they went out. "I didn't think I'd kept her talking long enough for you to get here," she said as they drove along.

"We only came when we did because Lynne rang the house to find out where Suzanne was. Luckily there's a phone box right opposite the farm, and rather than keep hanging about in the dark and cold she decided to use it. Thank heavens it hadn't been vandalized.

"Naturally, as soon as she rang I knew that Emma hadn't even set up the meeting we'd planned. Even then I didn't really understand why. I just knew that something must be wrong and Stuart and I dashed straight here."

"So you still didn't suspect Emma?" asked Claire.

"No. I thought she and Suzanne had been caught by the killer, not that it was Emma all along."

"You mean Emma wasn't even your second choice! It's a good job you're not going into the police force!" laughed Claire.

"How can you make a joke about it when you nearly died?" exclaimed Steven. "I feel absolutely terrible about the whole thing. How could I have been so wrong?"

"I don't think anyone would have guessed it was Emma," said Claire comfortingly. "I certainly didn't."

"But the chart made it look as though it had to be Lynne!" said Steven in frustration.

Claire gave a small smile. "You know what they say about figures and graphs: they can be made to say anything you want them to say."

The doctor looked over his shoulder. "Stop talking, young lady. You've lost a lot of blood and need to reserve your strength."

"My fault," apologized Steven. He bent his head closer to Claire. "We'll have lots of time to talk about it all in the future," he promised her. She nodded and closed her eyes. For the moment, she was content just to be alive and with Steven. Her other problems could wait.

Epilogue

It was Christmas Eve, and the remaining ex-members of the now disbanded Dorking Future Drama Group had gathered together at Stuart's house. It wasn't exactly a party – none of them felt that would be appropriate – but there were drinks and snacks. For the first time since Emma had vanished inside the walls of a hospital for the criminally insane, unlikely ever to be fit enough to be tried for the killings, they felt able to talk freely.

"The police certainly gave us a good going-over," said James as he wrestled with the pull-ring on his coke can. "They were so furious I think they'd have liked to arrest us all."

"You can't blame them," said Suzanne, her left arm and right hand still in plaster. "If Lynne hadn't had the sense to ring my house they'd have had two more corpses on their hands. Imagine what the public would have had to say about that!"

"I think it was me they really wanted to arrest," said Steven. "I got the lot: withholding information, wilfully obstructing them in the course of their enquiries. At one stage I honestly thought I'd end up in court."

"What did your parents say?" asked Lynne.

Steven gave a short laugh. "That's the ironical thing, really. My father said that since I was obviously a total idiot, acting was probably the only career I was fit for!"

"I really rang you because I was so cold," admitted Lynne. "The WPC who interviewed me kept saying how clever I'd been, but I hadn't. I never guessed anything was wrong; I thought Suzanne had simply forgotten me."

"I still can't believe it was Emma," said Becky. "To be truthful I thought it was you, Claire."

"Thanks a million," said Claire, sitting with Steven's arm round her shoulder.

"Well, you were always strange. Emma was so normal."

"Emma drew that skull when we were all voting, did she?" asked James.

"Yes. If you remember, Emma wanted to take art at school but it didn't fit in with her other subjects," confirmed Suzanne.

"That should have told me it wasn't Lynne," admitted Steven sheepishly. "You can't draw at all, can you, Lynne?"

"No. I'd have told you that if I'd known you thought I was a mass murderer."

There was a general round of laughter, although somewhat subdued.

"Was the whole plot really hatched in order to get rid of you, Suzanne?" asked Chris.

Suzanne shivered, and it was Steven who answered for her. "That's what Emma's still telling the doctors. Neither Suzanne nor I believe that she'd hated her for very long. It seems that she couldn't cope with family life once her mother re-married. She felt pushed out by Paula and wanted to be first with someone. That someone was me."

"Christine told me that Emma's father was prone to terrible rages," said Lynne. "That was the cause of the divorce, not another woman as Emma said. Perhaps it was something that was wrong with her all the time, a weakness like a heart defect that's lurking beneath the surface without you being aware of it. Then some tiny little thing triggers it off, in her case possibly Paula."

"I feel sorry for her family," said Claire softly.

"They've moved away," said Stuart. "Her mother wrote to Mike before they went, saying how sorry they were about Hazel and explaining that they thought it was better for Paula if they moved away and started afresh somewhere."

"I hope they never realize Paula was the trigger," said Suzanne. "Emma was always complaining about her, although I thought she was a sweet little girl."

"I don't suppose we'll ever know for sure what tipped Emma over the edge," said Claire briskly. "I think the time's come for us to put it all behind us. We won't ever forget, but we've got to get on with our lives now."

"Yes," agreed Stuart. "Although lots of people are saying she should have had to face charges in court, I think that's nonsense. She was mentally sick, and no trial would bring Richard or Hazel back. It isn't as though they're ever likely to let her out. She was extraordinarily cunning all the time. Why, she even joined the group of us who discovered that tape recording of creaks she'd planted."

There was general agreement, and slowly the group began to break up into couples and the topic of conversation changed.

Steven stood up and went to the french windows of the sitting room, looking out into the darkness of the garden. He wondered what view, if any, Emma had from her room in the hospital.

"What are you thinking?" asked Claire gently. "Dreaming about becoming Sir Steven Parkin one day? If so, I hope I'm Dame Claire Elliott first.

Now that Dad and Louise have agreed to put me through drama training, who knows? Perhaps I'll act rather than teach."

Steven put his arm round her. "Who knows indeed? But I wasn't thinking about that. I was thinking about Paula: I'm sure she was the catalyst. It was so strange, but when I was holding Emma that last day, she asked me to sing her a lullaby. At the time I thought it was just another manifestation of her madness, but now I'm not so sure. Perhaps all she wanted was the kind of attention little girls get: lullabies and bedtime stories."

"Perhaps it was," Claire agreed. "The point is though, we all have to grow up. No one can have lullabies for ever."

As the group of friends continued their evening together, Emma sat alone in her hospital room, softly humming to herself. The nurses were used to that. And they were used to the fact that she always crooned the same tune too: "One Hand, One Heart", from *West Side Story*.

POINT SF

Encounter worlds where men and women make
hazardous voyages through space; where time travel is a
reality and the fifth dimension a possibility; where the
ultimate horror has already happened and mankind
breaks through the barrier of technology . . .

The Obernewtyn Chronicles:
Book 1: Obernewtyn
Book 2: The Farseekers
Isobelle Carmody
A new breed of humans are born into a hostile world
struggling back from the brink of apocalypse . . .

Random Factor
Jessica Palmer
Battle rages in space. War has been erased from earth and is
now controlled by an all-powerful computer – until a random
factor enters the system . . .

First Contact
Nigel Robinson
In 1992 mankind launched the search for extra-terrestial
intelligence. Two hundred years later, someone responded . . .

Virus
Molly Brown
A mysterious virus is attacking the staff of an engineering plant
. . . Who, or *what* is responsible?

Look out for:

Strange Orbit
Margaret Simpson

Scatterlings
Isobelle Carmody

Body Snatchers
Stan Nicholls

Read Point SF and enter a new dimension . . .